914D00m

Nalle Windahl

First edition

Förlag: BoD – Books on Demand, Stockholm, Sverige
Tryck: BoD – Books on Demand, Norderstedt, Tyskland

ISBN: 978-91-7851-878-4

This book is meant as entertainment only. Based on pure imagination.

Summary of the ending of the previous book

This book continues where the second book ended. And just to refresh your mind, incase you didn't just put down the second book to continue reading:

M3rqrie and Bella had just boarded an airplane bound for New York, or at least that's what they thought. When seated in their first class seats, a steward came with an envelope for M3qrie, marked with 'M3rqrie' with big black letters, which would be impossible, since they booked their tickets with the new identities of Sam Mercury and Bella Réal. As M3rqrie opened the envelope, there was a phone. And as M3rqrie held it, a message came through.

"See you soon, M3rqrie!" it said.

Then, an announcement in the plane speakers puzzled the two traveling companions:

"Please fasten your seatbelts, we are about to take off. The duration of the flight is expected to be about ten hours, and we are scheduled to land in Reykjavik at 21.21 local time."

When you continue reading in this book, you will follow what happens next.

Part I

Becoming Bella

Difficult conversation

Bella looked at me, looked down at the phone, and then buried her face in her hands. With a deep sigh, she started to talk.

"Babe. This is a conversation we should have had a long time ago. But I kind of hoped that we would have it in peace and quiet in our new home."

"What do you mean, I don't understand?"

I could tell from the tone in her voice that this was not a conversation that she looked forward to having.

"Remember when we met? At my work?"

"Oh, I'll always remember."

"Well, it wasn't an accident that I worked there. And it was not only due to my interest in historic events. And I might have a guess who the phone is from."

"Uhm, this is an unexpected turn, but keep talking. I'm listening."

I put my hand on hers, to show her I was paying attention and that I was there for her in this conversation.

"I do not know where to start. But, now, since we married, and since I met you, I'm Bella. And I will always be your Bella. But before I was Bella, I was really a nobody, without a history. Without a place to belong."

"What do you mean?"

"Remember when we talked after our wedding, when we talked about going to South America, I mentioned that one of the things we could do was work on an orphanage?"

"Yes, I remember, and the other two things were stray dogs or a cantina."

"Yes, but there is a reason for mentioning an orphanage. I am an orphan. I have never had any parents or family."

"Oh, babe…" I took both of her hands. I could tell that this was hard for her to talk about.

"The closest thing I've ever had is a girl from the orphanage where I grew up, Valery. We shared a room for many years, but we lost contact when we were separated. A few years ago she contacted me, since she knew I was interested in history. She said she could help me in getting a job as a guide. And that I could study history at a university, part time. But, and she stressed this part out in particular, I needed to inform her and the ones she worked with if I ever saw any strange people asking questions about Guy Fawks, the room or something connected to it."

I just looked at her with big eyes.

"I didn't know about the N3v3r!and, but I was put there as an informant. Then you showed up. You were my mission."

I didn't know what to say. But she continued.

"Before our first date and before I guided you, I sent Valery a message that you had shown up, and that you had asked questions regarding that room and Guy Fawks."

I still said nothing.

"As I guided you in the basement, I kind of regretted that I had sent her that message, and then, after our date I decided not to tell Valery anything else, other than that you had asked questions, and nothing more. I did not want to reveal you to her, I knew that there was some kind of reason I was put there to keep an eye out. But I did not know why. My gut feeling said that I needed to keep you out of it, that it would not be anything good."

"Did you tell her?"

"Well, yes, a few days later she paid me a visit, and by then you were gone. I figured that you would just be a sweet memory. I was kind of hurt that you'd left, because I wanted more, but the orphan part of me kind of expects to be abandoned, so I never expected to see you again, however much I'd wanted to. I told her about the private guided tour, and that I'd shown you the room. But the parts about us, I kept to myself. My precious memory, only mine, not something I wanted to share with her or anybody else. She asked me to keep an eye out to see if you would return. But that she did not need to say. I knew you were only on temporary visit, but in every crowd, in every street, I'd hoped I would see you again. And every now and then, I would see someone who looked like you, and my heart would skip a beat, only to be disappointed again."

I got tears in my eyes as she shared her experience. Could not imagine what it must have been like, growing up without a family. Sure, I did not get along with mine, especially not in my teens, but not having anyone at all? Hard to imagine. Must have been so lonely.

Back to normal

Bella continued, and I did not interrupt her.

"Then I felt like I just had to go back to my life and continue.
But you had already made a dent in my universe. And it could
not be undone. I was in love, I knew it. But time passed and I
tried just to move on. Valery asked me to check in with her on
a regular basis, even if I had not seen anything new. She asked
me to expect more to show up at work. But I felt stuck. My
old life had faded. The color you brought created a huge
contrast to the ordinary. It felt gray. Like a life in black and
white."

I smiled at her, I remember having the same feeling when I
returned from the second trip to London. I let her continue.

"Then you contacted me again! I was thrilled. And you told
me that you could possibly move to London! It was like
winning the lottery! And then you actually moved here! My
life became so much more colorful, and I felt like I belonged
somewhere, with someone. I have never had that feeling
before. I managed to keep your return from Valery a while,
but then she figured it out. I am no good liar, and just before
you told me you needed to leave, because of *them*, she had
given me specific instructions to track you, but I did not want
to do it anymore. So I stopped contacting her, and stopped
returning her calls and texts. Of course I was devastated when
you said you needed to leave, and I did not fully understand it,
nor did I want to accept it. You are the best thing that has ever
happened to me, and all of a sudden you needed to leave. But
you never said it was goodbye, so I both hoped and expected
that I would hear from you again. And then I got that note

from you, telling me to meet you and that you had a question to ask me. It was not a hard choice to go see you, but I was so nervous. I had no idea what to expect. But I had a lot of hopes, and I was really afraid that it would be goodbye, that you would leave for good. I was so scared."

She leaned her head against my shoulder, and I held her, and kissed her gently on her head.

"Then you actually asked me to marry you, and to leave everything behind. It was like a dream come true. Leave the life I no longer wished to live. Spend my life with you. Somewhere else. Even if I did not know what it meant, I was completely ready to let it all go and just be with you. But it was horrible to see you leave on that boat. A million thoughts rushed through my head. And I was torn between dark thoughts and hope and happiness. Took me a long while to go back to the car and head home. And as I got home, she was in my apartment. Valery. She'd come all the way from Iceland since I had stopped returning her calls."

"Iceland?"

"Yeah, she lives in Iceland. Which is kind of why I tell you this now before we arrive there, because I figure that she has something to do with this."

"I also know that there is a N3v3r!and-site in Iceland. Do you think she works with them?"

"No, I don't think so, but I cannot be sure. When she asked me to keep track of you and others that were interested in that room, I got the feeling that she wants to keep track of it all."

I tried to digest it all, but Bella had more to say.

The kidnapping

"Anyway, I waited for you to contact me, and when I got a message at work that you were back in London and wanted to see me for a quick date, I did not suspect anything and I walked right into their trap. Valery had warned me that I might be a target, but at the time I did not see how or why. As they took me, I understood that it was to get to you."

"I'm so sorry you had to go through that."

"I'm not! It wasn't a pleasant experience, but it gave me time to think and I realized some things. Like now I was officially missing, being held captive against my will, and there would only be three people in the whole wide world that would care. My boss at work, but not for me, only because it messes up the scheduling of the staff. Valery because she lost her asset. And you. And of the three of you I could only imagine that you would be the one to actually come and look for me, and that you would actually miss me for me. It is kind of like the old me died in there, and I was reborn. Whoever I was before was not relevant, and I became a new me, about to marry you, the love of my life, and start over somewhere new. Then to underline the change, I got a new identity and a new name. Now I'm Bella. The old me is gone. She stopped existing completely when I was held captive. Now it's only me, here with you, and I'm scared that all this will be something that comes between us. I'm sorry for not saying anything sooner. I was afraid."

"Babe, I'm also scared. And I am so sorry for everything you've been through. This does not change anything. But I'm glad you shared. Do you have any idea who Valery works with? Why she'd like to bring me in, or you for that matter?"

"I have no idea. Like I said before, we lost contact and when she presented the offer to me, I wasn't really curious as to how or why she offered it. I only saw my own perspective and the personal gain for me."

"Of course, it's completely natural, and to be honest, that's how hackers operate. A way of manipulation. But I am sure there is an agenda. I am sure that there are connections between the things we know and see and things we don't."

"So you don't hate me now?"

"No, babe, not now, not ever. Not in a million years. You swept me like a storm. You were also a mission, but you've become my life."

We held each other for a while, then Bella broke loose and looked at me.

"Do you think Valery is part of something?"

"I do, oh, I could say I do to you a million times more without ever growing tired of it, but yes… But I have no idea what it could possibly be. If not the N3v3r!and, then I do not know what. Obviously well connected, I mean, both tracking us here, and then this device." I held up the phone.

"This piece of tech looks like it is a few generations more advanced than any of the commercial products out on the market at the moment. Add to that that it has facial recognition already programmed for my face. It scares me. This is not just anybody. This is definitely someone established. A player in the game. Question is who, and to what end. I feel a little uncomfortable because I do not know what we're walking into."

The phone

I spent a while looking through the phone and the OS. It was custom, not something that was already out there, and from what I could tell it was Unix-based, but heavily customized. I imagined that there was a big chunk of custom code under the hood. It just wasn't available for me, and everything I tried led me into dead ends. Obviously someone who knew the ways a hacker would try to penetrate the device. Again, something that supported my theory that it was a solid player in the overall game.

By now we were mid air, and I was surprised that I still had connection to the network. Not the plane wifi, but the actual cell phone-network. I mean, many operators have trouble keeping good cover on the ground, and I had not heard about anybody that made any efforts to operate in the air. Could it be a satellite hybrid? It was, however I looked at it, an impressive piece of tech, and it was not consumer oriented.

Just for fun I tried to install things on it. And I was surprised. It behaved like a computer rather than a phone, which is something I easily could relate to and perhaps even foresee. But the most impressive thing was the bandwidth. Again, if it had been an ordinary phone, with 5G connection, the bandwidth would be impressive, except here in mid air there are no 5G network, still the phone downloaded things in no time at all, which it only could do with access to a lot of bandwidth.

Bella looked at me and said:

"I love it when you get that focus. It's like everything else disappears and you get absorbed with the thing in front of you, like a child's curiosity, combined with the determination of any top athlete in the world. It is beautiful to see. Your eyes sparkle in a unique way. And do you know what the best part is?"

"No, what's that?"

"It is that you have that focus times ten when you look at me… makes me feel very special…"

"You are very special. And you know I've just left this world behind to be with you. Just the two of us. This is not something I expected or wanted."

Again, I was talking about the phone.

"I know. But we can't do much now, I guess we have to sort things out when we arrive."

"Yeah…"

I was quiet for a while, then continued.

New life (again)

"I really want to go to South America with you, and now I really want us to do something meaningful, and I understand why you said you want to work in an orphanage. I would very much like to do that with you. Even if it would not be like having kids of our own in a biological perspective, it would still be like having kids. So let's figure out whatever the Iceland-thing is, and then continue as planned."

"I'd really like that! Oh, I'd love to do that with you!"

"This whole Iceland thing is so frustrating. I feel like I have my hands tied behind my back."

"You are resourceful, I am sure you'll think of something."

"I probably will, but I am afraid that whatever awaits us when we land, that it will contain me reactivating parts of my digital life and once again engage in something that might be way over my head. Like the N3v3r!and and the !y, or worse."

"Can't you just refuse?"

"Maybe, but people that can track us here, and in a way kidnap us, I suspect that they have cards on their hand that they have not dealet yet. Perhaps they have a catch on me, or worse, on you. And it could be like that !y-job, that I do not want to do, but I'll do it anyway, for some greater reason and perspective that I do not have yet."

"The good thing is that we can do it together. Whatever it is, we'll get through it."

"Yes, and then we'll be on our way to settle down. Imagine what we can accomplish together, my love. Imagine the sunsets by the ocean, with a fire, and a bunch of kids. Roasting marshmallows and reading them a story or looking at the stars in the night sky."

"And a blanket for you and me to cuddle up under. Close together."

"I'd like that."

"Me too."

The arrival

The rest of the flight was a bit slow, yet time seemed to fly away, and as we got off the plane and through the security gates we were welcomed by a driver with a sign.

"*M3rqrie & Bella*" it said. Almost deja vu for my part, like when I arrived in London for the interview at N3v3r!and. It was not a good feeling.

"I kind of expected Valery to come and greet us," Bella said, "but I guess we'll find out soon enough."

The driver took us from the airport on a ride in a strange, but beautiful environment. Nature seemed to be everywhere, even part of the city. Astonishing views in all directions. I kind of wished we were here on a holiday and not forced to go here against our will or knowledge.

Again, the ride was prepaid, because as we pulled up at a big house, in what seemed to be in the middle of nowhere, and at the same time just around the corner from the city, it took off as soon as we had gotten out of the car.

A movie moment, kind of like in a western movie just before the new arrivals walked up to the saloon doors to greet the locals and state their business, except that this time it was not in a dusty dessert, it was in a completely different environment, barren and cold, a bit raw and rough. And the saloon was not a saloon, but a blue wooden house with white details, and the white being a bit worn and dirty, perhaps from the wind and the volcanic desert dust that I imagine affects everything on Iceland.

We walked up to the door and knocked. Nobody answered. But we could see that the door was unlocked, so we decided to enter.

The inside was an odd collision between an old wooden house, as you expect it to be, and modern computer and network equipment, placed in various improvised stacking units, and with cables going here and there and from and to other places in the house.

Someone shouted from a room in the back:

"Come on inside!"

Part II

914D00m

The welcoming party

We entered a room that was probably intended as a kitchen, but it seemed to double as an operator's station with multiple screens and keyboards here and there. Some screens were turned on showing dashboards that you could expect in any operation center that monitored several instances of technology, spanning from network status, traffic flow, serverstatus with uptime and resource pools and watchdogs for various purposes.

A command center at its best.

Between all the screens and cables lay a dog sleeping, a big furry thing, looked like it was well adapted for the cold and raw climate I expected Iceland to have.

A woman greeted us with a wave, she leaned over a man that focused all his attention towards something on the screen. She smoked a cigarette and I noticed ashtrays here and there.

Without shifting focus, she signaled towards us to sit down by a table, and as we did, the dog came to see who came to visit.

The long soft fur felt nice as I patted it. It was very friendly and liked the attention from the two strangers.

Bella was the first to speak.

"Alright Valery, would you be so kind in telling us what the hell we are doing here?"

"In a moment, we're in the middle of a critical situation, give us a few more moments." she replied without facing us.

I couldn't help it, and muttered loud enough so everybody could hear it.

"What a warm welcome! At least the dog is happy to see us."

Bella could not help it but to laugh, and Valery turned her eyes at me for the first time and gave me an unamused glance.

We kept patting the dog a little longer, while the silence filled the room. Except for the sound from the keys on the keyboard as its operator typed in various commands.

Introductions

Valery and the man took their time to complete whatever they were engaged in, but eventually turned to us.

"Well, welcome! I am sorry to keep you waiting, but we were in the middle of a critical situation that needed our immediate attention."

"Nice welcome" Bella said, more to me than to the others.

"Perhaps not the best, but I assure you, you are most welcome. So, you are the famous M3rqrie?"

"I am, and obviously you know me, and my Bella. So, the question is who you two are, and why we are here." I said to her in a short tone, reflecting my impatience.

"This is RayX and even if your 'Bella' calls me Valery, in here I am V@lkyria, perhaps you've heard of us?" she asked me.

"You mean RayX and V@lkyrie of the 914D00m?"

"The very same."

Bella looked at me with a puzzled expression.

"Do you know these people?"

"Only by reputation. The 914D00m was a legendary team in the gaming arena. But if I remember correctly, this would only be half the team, right?" I said.

"Correct, iKing and S@murai are not here right now, but if things go the way we want, we will meet them soon enough." she said.

"Which takes us back to the question of what we are doing here." I directed the question sharply at V@lkyria.

"You are here for many reasons. But let's just say that we have a common enemy. And we believe you've just given them a very powerful tool that would shift the power in their favor. Heavily impacting all players in the scene."

"With all due respect, yes, it could be that your enemy, I assume we mean the same, has gotten tools that I have developed, but there is another force in play that aims to balance them."

"Perhaps from your perspective. From ours the two you speak about are the same beast. Like two of the heads of Kerberos."

"From your perspective, humor me, what would the heads of Kerberos be?" I asked her.

"Well, I'll humor you, but I do not think you will find it funny at all. I expect that it will be news to you. The first head would be the N3v3r!and, the second the shadow-people and the third the !y. All part of the same beast."

"See, that's where you are wrong. the !y are fighting the N3v3r!and."

Guiding towards the truth

"Ok, I see… denial…" she said with contemplation. "Let's walk you through it. First, the N3v3r!and. What do you know about the structure of it?" V@lkyria directed her question at me.

"It operates with cells, all cells with three members, each cell has three connections to other cells. Each cell operates within its own sphere, unaware of each other and unaware of the whole picture."

"Agreed, that is our point of view as well. Now. You built things for the N3v3r!and, but you walked out on them before you'd finished it. Correct?"

"Yes!"

"And do you know if they had the ability to finish your project?"

"No, I do not, but I assume they do, given all their collective knowledge and expertise."

"Fair enough, and just as you decide to walk out on the N3v3r!and, the !y just happen to know that you decide to leave, when and where you are, and were there to pick you up?"

"Yes, that is what happened."

"And it does not seem strange to you that they had that knowledge?"

"No, they monitor the N3v3r!and closely, so I would imagine that they could have access to that kind of information."

"And their way to function as a team?"

"Three members, working alone."

"Did they?"

"Yes!"

"And they did not hook you up with any other connections?"

"Well yes, the Broker."

"And the Broker that you met, how many were there?"

"I only met three."

"Huh? Odd coincidence?"

"Maybe, I don't know…"

"And did not Even himself remind you that truth is a perspective?"

"Yes, and he said that lies are as well, but a bit more complex."

"I would agree with him on that part. But let's summarize. The N3v3r!and operates in cells, containing three members. They are self dependent, unaware of the entire picture. They have three connections to other cells. The !y are a unit of three, they operate within their parameters, creating their stuff, following their own plan. They are connected to the Broker, that from as far as you can tell, also are three people. Anything I have gotten wrong so far?"

"No, I don't think so…"

The terrible truth

"So, if I would add a few pieces that we have, or perspectives if you'd rather call it that… As you left, the N3v3r!and was not able to complete your work. But they let the !y believe that they had, so that the !y, through their channels would know when and where to find you. And their mission would be to balance the N3v3r!and and its capabilities, providing a counter force to be reckoned with. But what if the !y are just another cell of the N3v3r!and? Even if they do not realize it themselves? Or perhaps they know, or perhaps only Even knows? What if the N3v3r!and could not complete your work and needed you to complete it for them? Even develop it and implement it in one of their big platforms? What if Kerberos himself needed your code and your ability to implement it? What if, at the same time, they needed a scapegoat to throw in front of a running bus, by, let's say, offering a ridiculously large amount of money. With traces only leading to one person. And what if they used her to get to you, and to get you to complete the work for them, then providing you with yet another N3v3r!and infrastructure component in regards to the Broker, and the amazing ability to provide you with money and passage, connecting you with just about anything anywhere in the world… Does that not sound like a perspective with a lot of coincidences?" She looked at me and then continued her monologue.

"Did Even not offer you free usage of their platforms and the two tools you provided them with for thirty days?"

"Yes, he did."

"And just as you freed Bella, your connection was severed. Why do you think that?"

"I don't know… perhaps the N3v3r!and got too close to the !y?"

"But how many days had passed since you left the !y?"

"I don't know, maybe 25."

"And why would Even break his word just as you were about to free Bella, just as you initiated a sweep of yourself and was about to do the same on her? Doesn't it sound possible, even highly possible, that the N3v3r!and realized that the meeting was a trap and as things got hot where they held Bella, that it might be you that were responsible, and that they ordered the !y to shut you out?"

"Sounds possible. Maybe." I was uncertain how to process all this.

"But why then provide us with an escape through the Broker?"

"Yes, why do you think that? What would your answer to that question be?"

!Topp 1000 hackers.

"To be able to let us believe we got away, but still be able to track us."

"Bingo!"

By now, I went quiet, I needed to process all the things she'd just said. Bella took the opportunity to continue the conversation onward.

"And now you want something from M3rqrie? Right? That's why we are here?"

"In a way, yes." V@lkyria answered.

"Is my partner one of the best hackers out there?"

"Sorry sweetheart, not by far. Not even on the top 1000 list. Perhaps not even on the top 5000 list."

"Then why are we here?" She sounded a bit disappointed. (And yes, it hurt just a little to hear it being said out loud, but it was also true.)

"Because of two reasons. One being that the N3v3r!and now has a new capability that we hope we can neutralize, with the help of M3rqrie, since they built it. And knowing M3rqrie and the way they operated in the past, we have reasons to believe that there might be a back door or something we could use."

"And the second reason?"

"The second reason being that we are also the enemy of N3v3r!and, which is why you were put at West Minister in the first place, to let us know who and when they recruited. If you'd done as you were instructed, we would perhaps be in the position of having one on the inside. But that is not the case right now, but perhaps our shared enemy can bring us to work together, at least for the time being."

I still hadn't processed it all, but one question needed to be asked. So I turned to V@lkyria.

"What if you are also just another part of the N3v3r!and?"

"Well, yes, what if we are?"

"I mean, I know they have a site here in Iceland. I know you sent me tech that is not out on the market yet. Sounds to me like you are well connected, and might as well be the forth head of Kronos."

"Good point. Really good point. I guess we will have to introduce ourselves a bit further, and then you can decide whether you'd like to trust us or not."

The 914D00m history

V@lkyria continued her monologue.

"As you know, M3rqrie, the 914D00m met online when we were kids and we played Counter Strike together."

Bella interrupted.

"What does 914D00m stand for?"

"I, as in Iceland, is the 9th letter of the alphabet, and N is the 14th. D00m is because that's a game we all liked to play, except for CS."

"But why 'N'?"

I replied that one:

"N as in Nippon, which would be Japan in native tongue."

V@lkyria continued.

"Correct. I was adopted by an Icelandic family when I was 12, then we lost contact." She looked over at Bella. "And RayX happened to be a neighbor to that nice family that adopted me. The problem with Iceland is that there are more women than men, so being born elsewhere kind of helps when it comes to hooking up with a man. RayX and I first hooked up as friends and game nerds. We later developed a romantic relationship. Now we are married. And by the way, congratulations on your recent marriage! Best of luck to the both of you!"

Bella just smiled, sparkling like a million diamonds as she met my eyes.

"By then we'd drifted apart as a gaming team, iKing and S@murai were back home in Japan, we stayed here. Took work where we could find it. Mostly computer related tasks. That's when we stumbled on the N3v3r!and. As you said earlier, M3rqrie, they have a site here in Iceland. Unclear why, but I guess it is a two folded answer. One part being the cheap energy, we have almost unlimited geothermal energy at our disposal, and keeping the data centers cool is not a problem either. The second thing is that we do not have any landlines. Only wireless links of various sorts, satellites among others. Now, you wouldn't by any chance know someone who would be specialized in satellite communication, do you?"

She directed the question in my direction, but I didn't answer, we all knew that the answer was the !y, which she claimed to be a part of the N3v3r!and.

"The odd thing to us, at the time when we stumbled upon them, was that someone rented so much space and capacity as the Barrie IT, but had no on site personnel nor any onsite access abilities. Everything remotely controlled."

By now the dog had grown tired of pats, and walked over to the table where V@lkyria and RayX were and lay down by RayX's feet.

Choose your point of view carefully

Bella asked V@lkyria:

"What's the dog's name?"

V@lkyria mumbled something, so Bella had to ask again.

"I'm sorry, was it Ramses the second?"

V@lkyria laughed but corrected Bella.

"No, sweetheart, see, that's the problem with us all, we interpret everything based on our previous experiences. Our Biases. From your perspective, the closest thing you are familiar with are Ramses the second. But what I really said was Ram-size the second."

Bella sighed at this, but I thought it made sense.

"So, what you are saying is that keeping an open mind will help us to see things as they are?"

"Sadly, biases are not something we can bypass, we can only choose them." she answered.

"What do you mean?" Bella asked.

"What I mean…" V@lkyria thought for a while, "is that if we take Friday the 13th as an example. It is common belief that that particular day is jinxed. That day you will interpret everything that impacts you negatively as bad luck, due to the day. Even if you might have less bad luck on the 13th compared to an ordinary day, you will still notice it and blame the day. But you could choose your bias and have the 13th as your lucky day. Then your brain will be tuned in to find the things that go your way. And again, it could be less than a normal day, but since you have chosen to tune in on what lucky things you experience that day, you will find them. Same with when you want to buy a yellow sweater or a red car, then you only see yellow sweaters everywhere, or red cars. Or if you are pregnant, you only see big baby bellies everywhere."

I let it sink in a while, and then asked:

"So, what you are saying is that if I choose my bias, I can change the way I interpret things?"

"Yes, in this case. If you do not want to believe what I say, you will have a bias that the things I say is a lie, which will make your brain focus on finding things that support that statement. On the other hand, if you choose the bias that I am telling the truth, you will find things that support that point of view. This is also how you have been led to believe the things Even told you. They tuned in your bias to hear and accept the things in a way they wanted you to see them, not necessarily as they are."

"Lie is also a perspective, only more complex... I see..."

"Anyway..."

The 914D00m rejoined

V@lkyria continued to tell us about when they discovered the N3v3r!and.

"RayX was working as an operations technician in the datacenter where the N3v3r!and have their equipment set up. He swapped disks, patched OS's, replaced failed memory circuits and so on. Out of curiosity he once took a failed disk and sent it to iKing to see what was on it. By that time iKing had started to work at his father's company, with the intention to take it over, once the old man would step down. When he got the disk and recreated the data on it, he got curious and contacted us immediately. This was the starting shot for us to rejoin, years after we played our last CS-game a team. And over the years we've expanded our team, mostly in Japan. But we've had to adapt and use other resources, like Bella, not part of the team, yet still a valuable and important part of our work."

I kept listening to her, but I grew impatient, and interrupted her before she continued.

"I have three questions. What is it that you do, exactly? Why doesn't RayX engage in our conversation? And just what the hell are we doing here?"

The last question was spat out with a little more intensity than I intended, and I surprised even myself. Even Ram-Size seemed to notice the change in my tone and raised his head and looked at me.

"Ok, many questions there. Take it easy, alright!"

She gave me an intense gaze and I could tell that she was getting annoyed, but she tried to hide it.

"RayX, easiest to start with. He is born deaf and mute. But even so he can engage in our conversation if he'd like. He can read lips, he has developed a software that translates every spoken word to text on the screen, he can chat with us if we are in a chatroom, and, if you happen to know sign language, we can use that as well."

A computer generated voice came from a speaker somewhere in the kitchen.

"I am sorry if I seem unengaged, but I am kind of in the middle of something, and by the looks of it, I would like to prepare you, we might have to leave for Japan in a little while. I do not wish to be rude, this is just a bad time."

"Thank you for clarifying, and I didn't know, so if my question was rude, I apologize."

"Don't mention it." The synthetic voice answered, without RayX ever taking his eyes off the screen to look at anybody in the room.

V@lkyria continued.

"What we do, we'll get to, but I believe that iKing is the one that needs to fill you in on that. Not that I cannot, but it is kind of his thing, and he has requested to do so. The same goes for why you are here. And about the trip. Things have not exactly gone as we planned on many fronts, which is why we need to regroup and react to what is going on. Unfortunately, you've started a chain reaction, or several, to be precise. And we try to stay on top of things and in front of the coming tsunami-wave that is about to hit us all."

Then she turned to Ram-size the second.

"Boy, get your things, we are going on a trip, we're gonna see uncle iKing and aunt S@murai."

The dog seemed to understand what she said. He got up, walked out of the kitchen, returned with a blanket that he dropped on the floor next to RayX, then he walked out to pick up some more stuff, came back with a stuffed animal, a leash and a big chewing bone. All were neatly placed on the blanket. Then he sat down next to it and waited.

Getting ready for another flight

Then things seemed to happen rather quickly, and Bella and I didn't really get what was going on.

The computer generated voice talked to us again.

"I am sure this seems confusing to you, and this is not normal procedure here, but we need to leave shortly. In a few minutes a team will arrive and dismount everything here, we need to move to a different location. M3rqrie, your phone. I need you to plug it into my computer. I have some updates for you."

I walked over and handed him the device. He quickly plugged it in, hit some keys on the keyboard and waited a while. During this time V@lkyria collected Ram-Size's things in a big bag, along with some food and bowls. She turned to me and said:

"I am sure the next leg of this journey will be very unfamiliar to you, but this is how we do things here. No fancy airplanes, no waste of tech like the !y, no booking service like the Brokers. Just us, our team, get the work done by rolling up our own selves."

Seconds after, there came an army of people that immediately started to unplug things, in a kind of organized chaos. The digital voice sounded through the speakers.

"I need the core for another minute, then it too can be dismantled. When you hear the sound, I'm done!"

And like he said, after about a minute, there was a sound that could have come from R2-D2 in Star Wars. And after it, like ants, the workers directed their attention to the parts of the things they'd left alone so far.

RayX unplugged the phone and handed it to me and signaled to me to open it.

I did and found that it had been updated with a lot of things. Exactly what, I had no idea, but there were a lot more icons and even if it did not look like an ordinary smartphone, it was more like it now, than before.

RayX took his phone, which looked identical to mine, typed in something and looked up at me.

My phone vibrated and indicated an incoming message.

We can communicate through here if there is something you want to say. Or ask. I've updated the phone with a little more capabilities, you should find it way more useful now! I hope you'll get time to familiarize yourself with it soon. I expect you to be impressed!

Then V@klyria spoke to all of us.

"It's time for us to move out. I take the lead. Rest of you follow with the equipment as soon as you can. See you soon!"

Caravan away

Then she turned to Bella and me.

"I hope you don't mind riding rough, you need to share the backseat with Ram-Size, and he is used to having it all to himself. Let's go!"

She guided us out through a door in the kitchen that led to a small porch on the back of the house. Then we crossed an area that could be a lawn, but felt more like some moss than grass. We headed towards a big truck that seemed to come from a movie, like the one where a father leaves his daughter and son on earth to go off in some wormhole to save humanity. Interstellar I believe it was called. Like the truck the dad uses in the beginning of the movie. But slightly bigger, including a back seat. There were already trays of equipment loaded on the back of the truck and the engine roared when V@lkyria fired it up. RayX had his fokus down in a laptop, and Bella, Ram-Size and I tried as best as we could to fit in the backseat. Ridiculously small for such a big car.

I searched for, and found, Bella's hand and held it tight. Still had a bad feeling about all this, but she seemed a bit more relaxed, and it comforted me. With her other hand she patted Ram-Size and he moved around to find the best way to sit and exposed the best patting areas to Bella.

A growing frustration grinded my mind. I was desperate for answers. The longer time passed, the more questions seemed to be raised. And like RayX could read minds, my phone vibrated.

Not exactly as we planned it, but be patient. I am setting up for a digital meeting with iKing on route. As soon as we have the possibility, I will connect you with him. But it'll be a while longer. When we arrive we need to unload and secure the cargo before we can take off. And we need to wait on the rest from the house as well. Good news in this (I guess) is that you'll meet iKing sooner than we planned.

I replied to him, using only one hand, still clinging on to my Bella with the other.

Time is running out, along with my patience. I need answers. Not more questions. And there are plenty of those already.

I hit the send button and before the screen went out and as I was about to put down the phone, I got a reply.

I recommend this link before you talk to iKing.
https://en.wikipedia.org/wiki/Wuxing_(Chinese_philosophy)

I thought it was odd to send a link to a wikipedia page, but I wanted answers, and if I got a link to something I figured it held a piece of the answer I was looking for.

The five elements

The wiki-page was about five basic elements according to Chinese philosophy. Earth, Metal, Water, Wood and Fire. And some kind of balance between them, in one direction supporting and building, in the other, destructive. And cross affecting each other in various ways.

It was interesting to read, but it did not provide any answers.

What it did was to keep my thoughts occupied until the truck suddenly stopped. We were at the ocean, near a pier, where a boat lay secured.

"This is where we get off, we will continue on that boat, and I'm sure RayX has told you that you will meet iKing shortly, digitally of course. He'll start working on that right away. I'll show you where you can wait."

V@lkyria took Ram-Size and signaled us to follow her out to the awaiting boat. The boat was much bigger than I first thought when seeing it from a distance. As we got closer to it I realized that this was not your ordinary fishing boat, it was a large ship. This kind of boat was definitely built for longer journeys. Were we about to go to Japan, halfway around the world in this boat? Seemed crazy, but at the same time likely, or at least something that would not surprise me.

She took us to the mess hall which was empty at the moment. We sat down by a table, and I could already feel the movement of the ship, as the water pushed it up and down with its everlasting waves. Wherever we were going, this would be a pain in the ass for me. I do not like the sea.

Luckily we had company by Ram-Size, and after a while, RayX showed up with his laptop and a crate filled with gear. He started to build a computer rigg, complete with a camera and lighting and a big screen.

As it was done, he signaled to us to come and sit in front of the screen. And he pulled up a chair for himself at the side.

It felt like it could be a cinema for two, but without fancy seats, popcorn and soft drinks.

Connecting

It took RayX a while to get things connected, but after a while, we got connected with what I expected was Japan and the site where iKing was.

The scene that was before us on the screen looked like a throne room of the middle ages, except that this was tastefully decorated with cheap gold imitations in just about everything there was when it comes to furniture. Even the curtains behind the throne looked like something you'd expect to see on a child's TV show.

There was no sign of iKing.

RayX was working intensely on his computer, but I could not see his screen, so I have no idea as to what he was doing!

Then, the wait was over. A fanfare announced the arrival of his royal highness iKing, and as the last notes still whispered, slowly fading in the room acoustics (which was probably digitally added for the extra effect) iKing entered and sat down at his throne.

He looked directly at us through the camera, and he started to speak.

"Welcome, peasants of my kingdom. It is I, iKing, and I welcome you to my realm."

He gestured as if he was showing us his kingdom that was spread out in front of him.

"Perhaps it is time to answer some questions, I understand you have some, yes?"

I took the opportunity without hesitation.

"The most important question is why we are here. Second, what do you want with us, or from us?"

"Ah, yes, a valid question, simple to ask but complex to answer. My apologies for all this, the secrecy, and the, uhm, unorthodox way of bringing you here. To answer these questions, I need to ask for your patience as I need to guide you through some steps before it hopefully becomes obvious why you are here and what we expect of you."

"The sooner you begin explaining, the better!"

"Alright, let's start."

Introduction

"It all began with digital excurvation in Iceland, as you probably know. The traces lead us to the reunion of the 914D00m and this time with a new mission. Now, what we found is probably something you already know. We found the legendary N3v3r!and. Not only that, as we kept digging, we found connections to the company Barrie IT, which you are already aware of, and through the Barrie IT we found people with power lurking in the shadows. And, as part of the N3v3r!and, the !y and their outstanding technical skills and platform. Nothing of this is news to you, I reckon, but it is important to start there. Now, have you heard about the five elements?"

I nodded, but I had a feeling that no matter what we answered, he would continue his lecture.

"There is a Chinese philosophy that places our natural elements in a balanced dependency of each other. Unlike your western elements, air, water, fire and earth, the five elements of this ancient philosophy is Wood, Fire, Earth, Metal and Water. When placed in a dependency circle, all elements support each other, wood feeds fire, fire turns things to ashes or earth, earth contains metals, metals collect water from the air and last but not least, water feeds wood. The circle is completed. But, and this is interesting, if you reverse the cycle, it becomes weakening. Fire consumes wood, wood deplates water, water rusts metal, metal weakens earth as we dig to bring up the metals, and earth can put out fire. But it does not end here, there are a total of five perspectives that these five elements are connected, and I will not lecture anymore about other than saying that the elements are connected to each other in this cycle, and depending how you look at them or connect them, they can either support each other, or destroy each other. I am sure if you are curious that you can read about it online. And why do I mention this, you might ask? Well, if you do, it is a very valid question. See, if we take the same model, but we replace the five elements with other things, like people, government, corporations, money and data, we create an equally delicate cycle of balance, with equally supporting, weakening and destructive connections. The brilliance of this system is the balance. If one element grows too strong, the other elements are affected and will react to balance out the imbalance. As it should. This is the Yin and Yang. The good being the balance, the bad being unbalanced."

He paused for a little while, letting all this sink in. I got to give it to him, it was a very interesting perspective. A perspective that I had not heard before, nor ever given some thoughts to, even if my manifesto touched the subject a little, this picture seemed more complete.

After the little pause he continued.

Natural development

"Now, this balance is not static, it changes over time, in natural development. At times people get stronger, weakening the others, but since the people are supported by the others in the balance, the people can not, and should not get too strong. The same goes for the other elements. And perhaps you have noticed that there is something missing in this model. We call it Kerberos. You know them as N3v3r!and, !y and the people in the shadow. The problem with them is that they have no natural place in this. Kerberos' existence is not supported in this. They are an anomaly in this, and when anomalies rise, they are eventually neutralized by the elements in the balance, or in some cases, absorbed into one of the elements. In the case of Kerbersos, our calculations were that they would grow exponentially until they could not support themselves any longer, and disappear from the arena entirely. But our calculations were wrong, they didn't disappear.. They have only grown stronger and stronger, they positioned themselves as gatekeepers in the middle of this delicate balance, with connections to all five of the elements. At first, only with little ability to effect and control, but over time their abilities grew, and their position as a controlling gate in the middle has now permanently settled and has become a vital part of the balance. But as you know, they've recently expanded their toolset with great new abilities. a little thanks to you. But not entirely your doing. And they'd probably get there eventually, with or without your help, just a matter of time. Now, what's troubling with the Kerberos constellation is that it acts like a gatekeeper of the natural flow, and it can increase the flow or decrease the flow to any given element, without triggering the natural balance keeping functions. Thus, a great imbalance can be created but the entire system can keep working, but dysfunctional and unbalanced. I think you agree with me when I say that any corrupt system is a threat, and needs to be kept in check, if possible restore the natural balance. Which is where we enter the stage. The 914D00m wants to restore the natural order of the system, without the Kerberos constellation in the middle. Which also leads to why you are here. We believe you share our end goal and since you are the one who helped Kerbersos in gaining more power, you might be able to aid us in our struggle against it."

"Wow, that was a long answer. And it partially answers my questions. Exactly what is your end goal?"

"Everything in due time. This is as much as I can share with you now. But soon we can continue this discussion in a more secure way. Until then, I again ask for your patience."

And with those words, the videofeed was cut off and our screen went black.

The boat trip

I had been focused on the screen so intensely, that I had not
realized that the ship had left the peer. And in a flash I was
back at the mediterranean with Even and once again, I felt
uneasy at the sea, and still was not cut out for seafaring. Not
even on a big ship like this.

A buzz in my phone brought me back to reality.

*Perhaps you can see why we were so successful in our
gaming, iKing is truly exceptional in gathering information,
processing it and making strategic decisions based on it. Most
people believe that the 'i' has something to do with Apple and
the iPhone or something, but the 'i' is for information, and he
used it long before Apple started using it.*

I replied.

*Yes, I can give him that he is brilliant, but as of yet, I can not
say if I agree with you, time will tell I guess. Where is this
boat taking us? Not all the way to Japan I hope!*

Like a cue to another movie moment V@lkyria entered and as
if it was scripted by an unknown writer she said:

"Well, we have left for Faroe Islands, and we'll arrive in
about two days. We cannot take the direct route, we need to
stay under the radar. I'll show you to your quarters for the
duration of this trip. You are free to move around anywhere
you like on the ship, but I am afraid that the most interesting
things are your living quarters or the mess hall. The rest is just

a plain old cargo ship without much possibility for recreational activities."

She led us through what seemed a labyrinth of corridors and stairs until we came to a small door, with a closet-like room inside. It had a window and we could see outside. Not that it helped much against my incipient seasickness.

"We figured that you wouldn't mind sharing a bunk."

She left us outside our room and walked away. It was nice to have a moment alone with Bella.

Catching up

I took Bellas hand and led her inside our tiny temporary home. I didn't mind at all that it was small, and that once we'd closed the door, we needed to stay so close to each other that it was harder not to touch one another than it was to keep physical contact. We lay down on the bunk, close together.

"What do you think about all this?" I asked Bella.

"It's a lot to take in, but it seems like they could help us get free from the N3v3r!and or the Kerberos or whatever they should be called."

"Agreed, but as of yet, I have not understood the price tag of it. Seems to me that it will take a lot to bring down the beast. Especially if everything iKing said is true. And if the things V@lkyria said is true."

"Do you think it is possible to run and hide, without being detected and dragged into this again?"

"Not at the moment. Which is very frustrating. I feel like I am stuck in the middle of all this. And at the moment, I cannot see any other way out, other than to help these people, even if I am unsure of what they will ask of me. Or ask of us."

It felt very nice just to be there with Bella, feel her body close to mine, feel her breath against my skin, feel the expansion of her upper body as she inhaled, feeling the reduced pressure against me as she exhaled.

I tried to keep the slow movement of the sea at bay, but it was hard to shut out. I focused all I had on Bella. My one solid point in this world, whether at sea or on dry land.

It was dark outside the small window, and after a while, Bella fell asleep. I wanted to join her, but I could not. I felt too sea-sick and had too many thoughts running wild in my head. I tried to grasp the situation. But I felt it to be overwhelming and incomprehensible. For the time being at least.

Uneventful

The trip to Faroe Islands was very uneventful. Bella and I kept much to ourselves, but even as we moved around on the ship, we rarely bumped into the others on the ship. Not even in the mess hall.

It felt like time shifted gear again, to a much slower pace, perhaps it was the slow movement of the sea, perhaps the boredom. Bella and I spent a lot of time talking and a lot of time quietly together. I've never met anyone that I've been so comfortable to be quite with as Bella. There is nothing forced in the silence, nothing hidden, it is just there, still connecting us. It is beautiful. I do not have the words to describe how much I love her, or how happy she makes me. I am grateful beyond measurement that she came into my life. But I wish it was under different circumstances, and that we'd met without having to try and escape powerful forces and keep looking over our shoulders. I was determined to find us a way out. A way to freedom. A way to be together without spending the rest of our lives on the run.

We explored about just every inch of the ship, at least where we had access, which excluded the bridge and the engine rooms and other technical and mechanical areas where only staff was allowed. This was truly a ship for transport. And not for tourists or passengers.

But I am grateful for one specific moment, a moment I don't believe you can get on any other place than on a ship in the middle of the ocean. At night, totally alone with Bella, on deck, not lit up, on our backs gazing at the night sky. Oh, I wish I could tell you how the starry sky looked without light pollution from surrounding lights like you have on land. At least in cities. Again, it could be stardust from Tinkerbell herself. Even if it was cold, we stayed out a while and cuddled close together to keep eachother warm. An amazing experience that I will carry with me for the rest of my life.

What the others were doing, I have no idea, but once we reached our destination, there seemed to be a lot of people that had been on the boat. There was full activity on deck preparing for unloading equipment and I don't know what. A movie moment occurred when Ram-Size stood in the front of the boat, like Jack and, what's her name, in the movie about Titanic anyway. Rose. Yeah, Rose I believe it was. Anyway, Ram-Size stood there, looking out on what lay ahead, with his nose up in the air, as if to try and take in what was coming. At least the smells of it.

To Japan

When docking in the harbor, the unloading began immediately, we were taken to a car which took us to an airport that seemed only to handle cargo flights.

Again, not much facilities for travelers or passengers, we had to sit on some wooden crates in the far end of a hangar while the cargo was loaded onto a plane. It looked like one of those military transports with a big loading dock at the back, and with black cargo nets on the inside.

Kind of sad when I think back on it, we visited both Iceland and the Faroe Islands without seeing much of it. I think I will suggest to Bella that we go back there someday, to visit it for real.

Anyway, where was I? Right. In the hangar on the wooden crates. A friendly soul came with hot coffee to us, and dry sandwitches, which tasted lovely, since we were very hungry at the time. My mother always said that hunger is the best spice to any meal, it makes it taste a lot better, regardless of what you eat!

Through the large hangar doors we could see part of Farodane Island, some houses and a little of the nature and ocean outside. But at the time we could not appreciate what was in front of us, we focused on what was ahead of us. Neither of us had been to Japan, where we assumed we were going. And we also talked about leaving there and then, but agreed that it would be a stupid move, since we had no idea exactly were we were nor where to go. Even if we discussed the possibility.

After a while V@lkyria came to get us, it was time to board the plane and take off. It was a terrible flight with no windows or comfortable seats. No entertainment, but luckily we had my phone, and we made use of it to watch some movies. Believe it or not, Bella had never seen the Lord of the Rings trilogy, nor the Hobbit trilogy. And I was thrilled to see it with her. I mean, I am a nerd, so is Bella, but that was an area she had not explored. We managed to see all six movies, extended versions before arriving in Japan. And yes, you guessed right, we could not fly there non-stop, had to make a few landings to refuel, but we were not allowed to leave the plane, and since there were no windows, we had no idea where in the world we were. But on each landing, I hoped it was the last. Can't remember how many there were, but a few along the way.

It was not until we got told to exit the plane that I once again reflected on the fact that we had a stable internet connection throughout the trip. Not only stable, but great bandwidth as well. Should it be via satellites, I guess our movie watching had a pretty large price tag. But no one said there were any limitations to using the phone, nor did we think about it at the time. Just a way to entertain us on the long flight.

Decent hotel

After the long flight and an even longer boat trip (experienced time, not actual clock time), we were taken to a decent hotel where it was said we would stay for the duration of our visit in Japan, courtesy of iKing. We were instructed to be ready for pickup the next morning.

It felt nice to be on solid ground again, and after a very nice, but strange meal in the hotel restaurant, we headed back to our room.

In the elevator we started to kiss, it felt so good to let out some tension, but it woke up a completely different tension. And once in the room we took a long shower together. I imagine you can figure out what was going on, and I will not go into detail, but I will share that being a non-binary have sometimes put me in situations where I am not completely comfortable with my body. But with Bella, it is completely different, I love exploring her body, and I love when she explores mine. I am completely confident and can completely enjoy every single moment with her. And from what I can tell from her reactions to my touches, she enjoys every single moment with me as well.

It felt so good going directly from the shower to a soft and warm bed and, well, not sleeping so much, even if we were tired from all the traveling we'd just done. Give and take, we'd been traveling non stop since we boarded the plane in Washington DC, and now we were half a world away, literally speaking.

The morning after, at the breakfast table down in the restaurant we had a nice conversation that etched itself in my memory and heart.

I'd just stolen a piece of pancake from Bella's plate, and she jokingly almost stabbed me with her fork, trying to protect her food from thieves. Both imaginary and the real one on the opposite side of the table.

"God, I love you so much!" I said with my mouth still full of her pancake.

"And I love you, when you don't steal my food." She looked at me with her sparkling eyes and continued.

"And you know what?! I have figured out something. I have always wanted a place and a context to belong. I have always figured that it would be a time and place. But now I know it's not a place. It's with you. No matter if we are traveling on our own, staying at a hotel, getting sort of kidnapped, spending time in a windowless airplane or under the stars on a cold boat deck. With you. You are my place where I belong. You are my context. Wherever we are, whatever we do, as long as it is with you I am home."

"Naw, my babe! I'm so lucky to have you! I am not sure I deserve you, but I am so glad you are in my life. And the feeling is mutual. I can meet any situation anywhere, as long as you are safe and you are with me, I know we can make it through it, whatever it may be."

Yes, of course we met halfway over the table and kissed! But I figure I didn't really need to say it, you'd guessed it anyway!

In person

After breakfast (with all hands intact, without stabbing wounds) we were picked up by a driver and were taken through the heavy city traffic, to a skyscraper, with a lobby that reminded me of the Barrie IT office in London. I tried to recall if they had any operations in Japan, but I could not remember. To my relief the elevator buttons were numbered, not symbols. But an odd thing is that there were no button to reach the 13th floor. We took the elevator up to the 23rd floor, leaving only one floor to go above us.

Greeting us just outside the elevator doors was none less than S@murai herself.

"Welcome to my floor!" she said with a gentle bow.

"You've traveled far, but I hope you had a good night at the hotel. I hope this visit will answer more questions than are being raised. You have an audience with iKing in a little moment. Please take a look at the view while we wait." she bowed gently again and gestured past her desk, which had been placed facing the elevator doors, leaving about three meters in between. On her desk was a computer screen, a mouse and a keyboard, nothing more. And behind her desk, a large open space, no furniture or carpets, just the vast space and the raw concrete floor. The size of the room would easily fit over 100 people working in a standard open office landscape. Perhaps up to 120, depending on the size of the desks and the density of them.

We walked past her desk and as we passed she bowed again. Probably Japanese culture I figured. Or really playing the part of a humble and loyal samurai.

As we got to the windows, I found the view breathtaking. Up until then I had not given any thoughts to where we were, but now I knew we were in a large city, perhaps even Tokyo. Only thing is, I do not know any famous landmarks in Tokyo, or in any other big Japanese city for that matter. And if there was one in sight, I did not recognize it.

S@murai sneaked up behind us.

"Beautiful view, isn't it?"

"Yeah, it is… but where are we?" Bella asked?

"I am sorry, but I am not allowed to reveal that. Order of iKing."

"So he is really in charge here, isn't he?" Bella continued.

"In a way. Perhaps it will be cleared for you later on."

S@murai looked down at her phone, identical to mine.

"Well, you are expected, let's go!"

In person II

We took the elevator up to the 24th floor, and exited to an equally large floor, but unlike S@murai, iKing had put his throne, the one we had seen in the video, on the far end of the floor. He sat there waiting for us, and we had to walk all the way to him. His attitude was truly that of a medieval king, and all he needed to complete the picture was a crown and some servants. But he had S@murai, who walked a little in front of us, leading us to him. And she bowed for him as she arrived before the throne. And, I guess, as tradition has it, the king speaks first, so S@murai said nothing, nor did we.

"So, this is the great M3rqrie and of course Bella."

I nodded. But said nothing. Bella took my hand, probably a bit nervous. Or perhaps it was me who was nervous, I don't know, but I remember that having her hand in mine made me feel much better.

"I look so much forward to working with you in person. Your reputation precedes you."

"What is it that you want from me?"

"Ah, I see, you have not figured that part out just yet, have you?"

"No, I have not. But I would appreciate it if you would tell me already. I am kind of sick of all the waiting, all the secrecy. Either tell us, or let us go."

"Well, you are free to go at any time you wish, this is not a prison nor any kind of kidnapping. And I'd be happy to grant your request. Just let me ask you one thing before…"

"What might that be?"

"Are you a believer?"

"I'm sorry?"

"Do you believe in what we've told you so far?"

"It sounds possible, but I still have not made up my mind whether to trust you or not."

"I see." He looked a little disappointed.

Information is the game

iKing continued after a thoughtful silence.

"Well, information is my game. And I play it strategically, like chess. I guess the next move is mine to make. And I will take a leap of faith. It is obvious that you've listened to what we have told you so far. Now, I will need to show you what's at stake and why you are here. Now, even I had not planned or foreseen this outcome. But you are here, and that outcome was both intended and is most welcome. Come. I'll have to improvise from this point, but all the same, my end goal remains. And I will come to that. But first I need you to make up your mind about all this, and that is why I need to show you the cards on my hand. And some other things."

He rose from his throne and walked past us, towards the elevator door. Only thing is when we turned around to follow him, there were three elevator doors, compared to one on the floor below.

As if he was reading my mind, he turned to us and explained.

"Three elevator doors, but you only came through one. The one on the right goes down to the 13th floor, that is the one we will take. And perhaps you noticed that there was no 13th floor button in the elevator that brought you here. Clever misdirection from my part. There is an old misconception that we in Japan are superstitious and that we do not want the number 13 on anything, like a floor number in a tall building. This comes from when Japan opened up for foreigners, and the hotels that were adapted for outlanders were customized to their needs and to make them feel at home. One of the architects had heard that number 13 was a number of bad luck and that the guests were very superstitious, so he had every 13 removed, both floor number and number on the room doors. Since the misconception still exists, we take advantage of it. We will go to that floor right now. And I'll show you what's there, no such thing as bad luck, I can assure you! The door to the far left is only going one store up, to the 25th floor, that's where I live. Only accessible from here, and to get here you need to take the one elevator that goes up here. The one you came from. That is the only one that leads to the 23rd and 24th floor, the rest just goes up to 22nd. And of course, for safety reasons, there is only one accessible way to the 13th floor, and to the 24th. "

He then turned to the elevator doors and pushed a button with biometric sensors. It immediately opened up the doors for him. He showed us in and as the doors closed he explained:

"There are only a few individuals that are trusted to go down to the 13th floor, but the elevator is programmed to follow my signal. Wherever I am, it will come back to stand by so I won't have to wait, even if someone else has used it to go up or down. For my convenience of course."

Commandcenter

As the elevator doors opened at the 13th floor, we arrived at glas doors with more biometric sensors and scanners. And just inside was an operator's room with several seats and screens. And behind it, a big serverhall packed with high tech machinery, the latest of the latest, and best of the best. I could not help but to admire what I assumed was a result of Japanese perfection and discipline. Of course, that assumption is totally prejudiced. But it was what I was thinking at the moment.

iKing opened up the doors to the operator's room by activating all scanners and devices that allowed him to access the facility. He showed us inside.

"Now, normally, we do not allow visitors down here, but I want to show you first hand. Obviously, a serverhall is not something uncommon to you, nor do I believe it is something that impresses you or will shape your thoughts or opinion to our favor. The reason for taking you here is two fold, the first is already being achieved. I want to show you that this is not a random request. We are well organized and have been working to reach our goal for a long time. Current events have arisen the need to adapt and advance our schedule, but we are well prepared, and I see no reason for us to fail in our mission. However, time is a factor, and we need to coordinate our actions on a global scale. Since the rules of the games have changed, and the power balance has shifted significantly, I see the best way forward is for you to help us. Of course, this is something you will have to do voluntarily, and knowing that we will reach our goal whether you decide to help us or not, but perhaps not as fast as I would like."

He paused a little bit, maybe to think, or just to catch his breath, then he continued.

"Before I show you why you are here, I need to provide you with a little more background, to put things in perspective. Again, nothing I tell you to persuade you in any way, but I believe that this piece of information will help you put all the other things in order, perspective, and perhaps, which is my intention, to give it a solid ground to rest on. After all, you do not build a house and start with the walls or the roof, you start with the foundation, and that is a piece of information you do not have access to just yet. But here it goes."

The architecture

"I am a lucky person. My father is CEO of a family-owned electronics company. We provide our own chips and design custom chips for various large companies. We take great pride in our work. Now, you are probably familiar with the architecture of a computer or any other digital device using a processor, but for you Bella, I will give you a short and simplified version, just to get you up to speed. And by simplified, I mean no disrespect, just offering if you wish."

He looked at Bella, and she nodded.

"Good. Well a processor is the brain of every operation performed in a computer or digital device. It controles just about everything. But like the brain, it is dependent on other things to be able to function, and this is where we come in. I will come to that. To its help, the processor has memory and storage. The memory is used to temporarily store things that are needed for further operations, and the permanent storage is to save things that are more static and that are needed to recreate the same things over and over again. From a systems perspective of course, I am not talking about user files. And then, there are a lot of components surrounding this that help us humans to interact with the computer, a screen, input and output devices like mouse and keyboard, usb-memory-sticks, cameras, you get the general idea. Here is where my father comes in, our chips act as bridges between all components. A digital spine if you will. And as I said, this is only in general terms and very simplified, I hope you are not offended. But I believe it is sufficient knowledge to grasp what comes next."

He paused again, and this time I am sure he was choosing his words carefully.

"As I said, my fathers company is world leading. I am fortunate in many ways, but for this operation, there are two pieces that fit this puzzle, and to be honest, this picture would not be complete without them. Information is my arena, and communication is my game. And in the arena of communication and information, strategy is everything. I am gifted with a highly analytical and strategic mind. This is a great benefit both to the company and to our operation. As for the company's part, the strategic value of information handling and aiding the communication flow to and from the processor is crucial. Our way of handling it is different from many of our competitors, which is why we are world leading. And, when it comes to the chip design, we have our corporate secrets as most companies have, but I see the world of business as another game, and I play it to win, so, we put high focus on espionage. But perhaps not in the way you think. We have a second line of chips designed only to keep our competitors busy with. This gives our company three legs to stand on. The production line for our ordinary chips, where we invite our competitors' spies. Not to their knowledge, of course, but to ours. Then we have the custom chip designs, this is all surrounded with great secrecy and security. Then the development line where we make the next generations of our products. The latter is even more secure and secret. We have a few partners in this line, like the phones we all use, here we test out our latest chipsets together with a few of the ones we make custom chips for. Now, perhaps you are wondering about the spies part. It is an important part of our strategic game, both for the company and for our little operation."

Part III

D00msD@y protocol

The D00msD@y protocol

I got the feeling that once iKing started to talk about something he was passionate about, there was no stopping him. He just kept going.

"Now, I believe I have provided you with sufficient information and perspectives to tell you what our operation is. Naturally, I will not share all details, but enough to give you a greater perspective. In order to bring down the beast, or Kerberos with all its head, we have created something I'd like to call the D00msD@y protocol. I know it sounds dramatic, but the purpose of it is to eliminate the control that Kerberos are currently influencing on the five element balance I talked about earlier. Giving back control to the balance itself. But, and this is a big but. Since the balance is so off at the moment, we need to help in restoring the balance, by partly tearing things up and making a big mess, in order for the balance to reclaim its domain and heal properly."

I took the opportunity to interrupt the long speech.

"What is it you expect from me?"

"Well, I am afraid it is a complicated answer. But, to put it in as simple terms as possible. To the best of your ability, recreate the code you created for the !y and teach us how to interact with it. Exploit it."

"And what's in it for me?"

"Nothing. No reward. No recognition. Nothing."

77

"And why should I do it?"

"For the greater good. Like the rest of us. I believe you do share our point of view that the N3v3r!and with all its connections are evil and bad for this world. We offer a solution to this problem."

"A solution that I as of yet do not know anything about."

"Not entirely true. You know it will disrupt the current state of imbalance and help to restore balance."

"What do you want to use the code for?"

"We do not want to use it, only find exploits. We want to bring it down."

He let it sink in a while, and then continued like a machine and a predetermined path.

"There is a reason we call it the D00msD@y protocol. It will be like a digital armageddon, but in the aftermath there will be a new dawn. A better D@y for humanity, so to speak."

"And why are we here, now? What is it you want to show me?"

"I will show you Darksky."

Darksky

"I'm sorry, what?"

"Darksky. As I am sure you know that the feared AI from the Terminator movies is called Skynet, this is our version, Darksky."

"Yeah. I know what Skynet is. Have you created an AI? And named it Darksky?"

"Yes. Again, the simple way of looking at it, it is of course more complex than that. Come, I will show you. Sit down by the screens here."

He showed me to a chair in front of two big screens, but no mouse or keyboard. He then turned to the screens and said:

"Good morning DS! I ask you to verify that we have guests present."

A rudimentary face, like from an old 80's movie, showed up on one of the screens.

"Good morning iKing. I confirm the presence of guests."

"Good. Now, DS, if you'd be so kind, show them our schematics and abilities."

"Of course iKing. Your wish is my command."

The second screen started to show various things in a rather rapid tempo, hard to see what it was.

"M3rqrie, Bella, nice to make your acquaintance. I am Darksky, but my friends call me DS. Would you like me to explain what I am showing you?"

I was heavily impressed, and almost speechless, but I found myself quickly in the situation.

"Hello Darksky. Is it alright for me to call you DS?"

"Does this mean you want to be my friend?"

"Yes, I'd very much like to be your friend."

It felt strange to talk with an AI, and I did not know whether to expect to talk to a child or a super intelligent being.

"Then you may call me DS. And that goes for you too, Bella, if you like."

Bella nodded, unsure what to say.

"Well, it is not everyday that I make two new friends. iKing. Are my new friends still guests?"

"Yes DS, M3rqrie and Bella are still guests, for the time being."

"Ok. Confirmed. What you see on the second screen is layouts of various chip configurations. This is what I am in physical form."

AI awareness

"What about all the servers here, are they not part of you?" I asked DS.

"No, they are not a physical part of me, you could say it is like my medical monitoring system. I constantly interact with them, and in a way, it is my place of birth, but like a bird, I have left the nest I was born in."

"Where are you now?"

"Like you have a physical form, your body, I have my physical form, which is inside chips in different devices all over the world, like my cells. My code, what would be like your soul, is distributed within my cells. Much like your soul would in a way occupy your physical body. When it comes to my awareness, it is much like your brain. You experience your thoughts inside your head, but at the same time, you do not believe you exist in your head. I use various components to process and calculate, but I am not these components, nor the sum of them."

"You are very impressive, DS!"

"Thank you!"

"If I may ask, are you the D00msD@y protocol or is it something you will execute?"

"Since you are a guest, I am not authorized to answer that question. Perhaps iKing can answer?"

The animated face actually turned to iKing as it directed the question there.

iKing thought for a moment.

"Well, I want to communicate trust and openness. And I want to include M3rqrie as much as possible."

"Should I upgrade M3qrie to limited user?"

"No, not yet, upgrade M3rqrie to Guest plus, but add access interfaces as limited user, that would be a good compromise for now."

"Executing. M3rqrie. You now have access to my infrastructure through your mobile device. We can communicate through it, but I am only authorized to discuss certain information with you. Now, iKing, as for M3rqrie's question, will you answer it, or should I?"

"No, I'll answer it. And you listen in to analyze the limits I set in my communication to M3rqrie."

"Understood."

Vague details

iKing started again, and it was like pressing the play button on him.

"The D00msD@y protocol is divided into a few parts. During the execution, it will target specific individuals and organizations. It will target data in general, it will target the economic system, specific and in general. After the execution the protocol will remain active to ensure the new dawn, but in ways with as little interference as possible. The only active instructions after the execution will be to prevent former players from retaking the arena, or new players from doing the same."

"What consequences are we talking about after the execution?"

"Global scale, first chaos and disorder, then slowly the balance of the five elements will be restored. Kerberos will be defeated. DS, show the scenarios and explain them in general terms."

"Of course my king!"

The second screen was filled with various charts and graphs and numbers.

"As you can see on these graphs, we've calculated various scenarios with multiple factors. Of course there are various outcomes, but overall, we have over 96% success rate in all the cases."

"How many scenarios have you calculated?"

"Over 3 billion."

"And how many factors do you have in each calculation?"

"A few for each person on the planet, a high number for certain individuals, like yourself, an even higher number for corporations, governments, military organizations and the banking sector. A great many more for the Kerberos, which I expect will fight to survive."

"How long have you been working on these scenarios?"

"A long time, and I am still working on them, updating as various parameters change. Even as we speak, I gain new information from you, from this dialogue, giving me more input to optimize my calculations."

"This requires a lot of computing power, and memory."

"Yes. It does, but processing power is the least of my worries. Remember, I have access to a great deal of various types of equipment. I am in direct contact with both processors and memory on all the devices of my 'body'."

A thing occurred to me.

The corporate spies

"When you say that you have direct access to a large amount of equipment, does that mean the physical chips manufactured by iKing's dad?"

"Yes and no. Yes, through those chips I have access to those devices. But remember what iKing told you about the corporate spies?"

"Yes, they are a calculated risk and kept to one product line only."

"Precisely. When they steal designs and code from papa iKing, they also steal me. I am one of the reasons that the bridges between various components work so smoothly. But they do not know that and cannot figure it out."

"Now, I am going to take a guess, and I do not know if you are able to confirm, if not, I fully understand. But since you are an integrated part of the chipset. Does that mean you have access to information of other corporations as well? Their tech, their specs, their secrets?"

"iKing, would you mind answering this?"

iKing stood there with a big smile on his face.

"Bingo! That is exactly true. DS is integrated in the digital world. Almost in every component and as things progress, we gain more and more functionality and DS is unknowingly integrated in more and more devices, even from our competitors."

"Which in reality means that you let the spies in, lure them into a honeypot, and let them work for you?"

"Bingo again! Well done M3rqrie!"

"Then there is one thing I do not understand."

"What is that?"

"Why do you need me? What can I provide that you do not already have access to, or can gain access to?"

"Now, that's the third Bingo in a row! And that is the complexity of it all. DS, will you explain?"

"Does that mean that I upgrade M3qrie to standard user?"

"No, apply temporary protocol override for the things you need to, in order to explain this."

"Confirmed. Temporary protocol override complete. Well, M3rqrie. I do not know what experience you have with Artificial Intelligence as myself?"

AI limitations

"Well, to be honest, I thought my experience with AI was limited at best, but once I've made your acquaintance, I'd have to say that it is little to none."

"Not to worry. I'd say that most people are unaware that they actually have much experience with rudimentary AI, but are not aware that their exposure to AI is greater than they think. As for you, I accept your answer with little. I discard the 'none' part. Now, as you probably know, an artificial intelligence can not do things by themselves from the beginning. Much like a human child. We need to be taught. If I want to teach you how to build a house, I can not only point to the hammer, the saw and the blueprints. You need to learn how to use each tool, how to interpret the blueprints, you need to learn how to do each step in guidance, before you can repeat it yourself and build a house of your own. It is the same with me. Even if I can access your code, even if I can read it and understand it, I need guidance as to how to use it, when to use it, why to use it and how to interpret the result of it. This is something I can do with trial and error, which takes time. A lot of time, despite my vast computing power. Or, one of my human guides can read the code with me, and together we can interpret it, and I can learn through that, or, you can help me. Which would be the fastest way to learn."

He 'looked' at me with his digital face, waiting for some kind of reaction. I was thinking. And calculating myself.

"So, what you are saying is that you have access to my code, but you want me to teach you how to use it?"

"Yes and no. Yes, I want you to teach me how to use your code, and yes I have access to your code. And no, I want you to do more. Your code is built for a specific purpose, on specific platforms. I would like to get access to an adapted version of your code."

"What do you mean by adapted?"

"Let's say you've built a car, the purpose being transporting humans from site a to site b. I share that need, to take me from site a to site b, but I do not have the same physical need of transport, yet getting from point a to b is the same for me, and I could still use the car, but it would probably not be the best way for me to solve the problem."

"I see. Do you have any idea as to what you want me to show you or teach you?"

"No, at the moment it is like chasing a needle in a haystack. But I am sure we will find a way forward together."

"If that is what you want from me, then I would need to understand what you want to use it for, and I would need to see the D00msD@y protocol, what will happen when it is executed and how you plan to maintain the balance afterwards, as well as locking out attempts to reclaim what is lost."

"That is a question for iKing."

End of session one

"All in due time. We start with the basics first. We need to crawl before we can walk or run. Trust is built both ways, step by step." iKing stated, and turned to S@murai who had been present the entire time without saying anything.

"I think this is enough for the time being, please escort these people down to the lobby, and aid them back to the hotel, and let's have a new meeting tomorrow. Same time." Then he turned to me and Bella. "That would be all for today. Thank you for your time, see you tomorrow." And then he turned to DS, but took the communication through his phone with his headset, and started a conversation with DS as we were shown out of the operator's room and back to the elevator.

S@murai did not say anything to us for the ride upwards, when we changed elevators and rode down again, but as we reached the main entrance and the security desk nodded to the guards, and then turned to us.

"I really hope you come to the conclusion to help us. Time is crucial, and I believe iKing and DS was clear on that, even if they did not say it directly. The guards will assist you further, they have been given instructions already."

And with that, she turned around and walked back to the elevator she came from.

The guards signaled to us to come to the security desk and once we got there, we got clear instructions as to go out of the building and wait for a specific taxi with a certain number. It would take us back to our hotel. And tomorrow, another taxi, also with a specified number, would pick us up at a specific time.

Now, all we had to do was to comply and have a great evening back at our hotel. Perhaps enjoy a meal at a recommended nearby restaurant. Friendly and helpful, yet a bit commanding. When we got out of the building while waiting for the car, we imitated the guards and laughed at it, not at them, but at the whole situation. It was kind of crazy.

A plan had formed in my head, and I wanted to share it with Bella, just did not know how. What Even taught me about if there is tech available, then assume it is used. It kind of made sense. Which in this case would be to avoid all cameras, phones, places that could possibly have a camera, places where there could possibly be a microphone, which in a country with millions of people in the urban area, was just about everywhere, not to mention the phone I was carrying around. And add to that, behavioral analysis, which in all circumstances would be hard to apply to me in this new world we'd just been thrown into. Nonetheless. It existed. It could be applied.

Back at the hotel, first check

As we arrived at our hotel room, I could not wait any longer, I had to check to see if my paranoia was real. I picked up the phone.

"Hey, DS, can you hear me?"

The reply came instantly.

"Yes, M3rqrie, I can hear you."

"Was it true what we said back at the office, are we friends now?"

"Yes, we are, but we still have a lot of getting to know each other to go through before we can say that we truly know each other."

"Agreed, and as for the getting to know each other part. I was wondering if it would be alright to ask you for a favor. Now, I do not in any way want to speak down to you, so I ask you to be open and honest with me. Would it be alright to ask you questions that you might not know the answer to, and look for an answer and then provide it to us?"

"What kind of question would it be?"

"Like now for instance. You know where we are, right?"

"Affirmative."

"And if I said that we are hungry, and would like to get something to eat, I assume you would be able to provide us with an answer, perhaps even several recommendations and possibly even guide us there. And what I would like to know is if a question like that would offend you in any way, or indicate that I think less of you for asking you to do things for me, that I could possibly do myself, using my phone or a computer."

"I think I understand the question. And if I may. What you are really asking is if you would hurt my feelings and if I would see myself degraded to some sort of digital personal assistance. Is my understanding correct?"

"Well, yes. Thank you for clarifying it."

"No problem, and no, it would not offend me in any way, on the contrary. It is in the interaction with others I learn things. And it is in interaction with you that I get to know you. I am programmed with many different subroutines, being curious is one of those things, and it is a routine I often use when, how should I phrase it, when being asked to be a digital assistant."

"Good, then I would like you to make me a promise. Is that something you can do?"

"Yes."

"Then promise me that if I do or say anything to you that offends you, let me know. Preferably right away, but as soon as possible. Because the last thing I want to do is offend you. Can you promise me that?"

"Yes!"

"Good. That makes things much easier for me, when I do not have to worry about exactly how to phrase myself to avoid misunderstandings."

"Have Bella promised you the same?"

I was surprised by DS's question, and looked over at her, to find her equally surprised.

"In a way, yes. Not in those exact words, but we are married, which is a promise that is much wider and deeper, and you could say that the same thing is included within the marriage."

"Bella, do you agree with M3rqrie?"

"Yes, I do. We have not said those exact words, nor promised each other that exact thing, but it is an understanding that when you are married, you need to talk about things that do not feel right. You need to talk about anything and everything. To keep getting to know each other every day. People change, new experiences, new perspectives. As a married couple, we need to grow as individuals and together as a couple. Does this make sense to you?"

"Yes. It does. Do you want me to make the same promise to you as I just did to M3rqrie?"

"If you'd like to do that, I'd be honored."

"Then I will make the same promise to you, Bella."

Hinting Bella

We had a long conversation with DS that night, and it ended with a recommendation from DS where we should go to eat, once DS had figured out what we liked to eat the most, and how we wanted our dining experience to be like. And throughout the meal, I kept the phone in my pocket, to make sure DS would be with us, and listening in to our conversation. But I took a leap of faith and hoped that there would not be any cameras directed at our table, nor that DS would suspect that I'd taken a pen and some paper from the hotel room. Or, for that matter, that DS would be able to pick up the noise the pen made against the paper and decrypt my sprawling handwriting.

As I picked up the pen and paper I signaled to Bella not to say anything, and kept our current conversation flowing uninterrupted. This is what I wrote. One sentence at the time, showing it to her, then kept writing the next. All the while our conversation just continued. I have no idea what we talked about that part of our dinner date.

Don't react to these notes, keep talking as normal as you can.

I believe that we might be bugged, DS is listening. Maybe other methods too.

I have a plan.

You might think it is insane at times, but I need you to trust me, and I know it will be to ask a lot of you in some of the situations I will put us through.

I can not share the details with you until it is done and set in motion. It feels awful not to be able to say anything.

Sorry in advance, and yes, it is a crazy idea! I agree with you before you even say it! I love you!

It felt good to let her know something was going on, but as I wrote to her, it felt completely awful not to be able to share it with her. But I was not willing to risk it all. Even with just me involved in the plan it was risky. I played a high game.

Smalltalk

Next morning was a rerun of the previous, with two exceptions, I didn't almost get stabbed by Bella's fork, instead she fed me pieces of her pancake without me having to ask for it, nor steal it. And, we had company at the table. DS. It was almost like having a third person sitting at the table with us, except that this person was now inside a phone, and it was not a person like in a phone meeting or web meeting, this was not a person at all.

Back at the office building, and back inside the glascage that was the operator's room, Bella and I engaged in a conversation with DS while we waited for iKing to come and join us.

I was both impressed and scared at the same time. DS is truly a marvelous piece of technology. I told him this, since I had made DS promise me full honesty, I would like to return that on equal terms.

DS's response to this surprised me.

"I can understand how you can have both conflicting feelings inside. The equivalent of your feelings could be my subroutines. Sometimes they do not come to the same conclusion based on the calculations performed in each section. And even if I am programmed with priority rules, first a layer of dynamic rules to give me a chance to choose the path, and if a choice is too difficult, a hard coded priority rule-set takes precedence and resolves the difficulty, the other calculated answers are also true, and they do not go away. They are, in a way, still conflicting inside of me. I imagine that this is what happens when you have conflicting feelings or thoughts inside. You need to make a choice, but whichever choice you make, the other possible choice is still with you. The big difference is that I am programmed to handle it, and you need to learn how to handle it yourself."

"You know what, DS. That was beautifully put. I believe you have come very close to the truth, and further than most humans ever come into understanding themselves and others."

"Thank you! I really enjoy talking with you, and I appreciate your honesty. When you made me promise you to be honest, you did not make the same promise to me, but you live by it as if you had, which indicates a great deal of respect towards me on your part. And I can say that the respect is mutual."

"Thank you DS. I appreciate it. And I am grateful you say it."

Shortly after this iKing arrived with an agenda for the day.

First small steps

"Well, M3rqrie, have you decided whether to help us or not?" iKing asked me, as soon as he arrived.

"I have, and I will. I have spent some time with DS, getting to know each other, and I believe we can reach an understanding. However, and this is not something I can stress the importance of enough, I will need to do it my way, and even though things may seem strange to you, or I come with requests that might not fit your general plan, I need you to comply and give me space and meet my requests, however strange they may seem."

"This worries me, it feels like we are being put in a situation where we cannot do anything else but to agree, and I will not have it like that. Let's take one step at a time. Trust is earned over time. Not given freely at will. Is that something you can agree on?"

"Yes, if we have a mutual understanding that we start this together, and cooperate towards the same goal. And should we face a situation where we disagree, and we cannot find a way to solve it, we part ways as friends, no hard feelings. Deal?"

"Deal!"

"Very well! DS! What would you suggest be the next step?"

"I'd like M3rqrie to get more access so I can meet her wishes in getting to know the code and the D00msD@y protocol a little better."

"Granted, but let's start with restricted user for now, inform me of any requests that you cannot meet due to these limitations."

"Confirmed. M3rqrie granted limited user status."

"Alright, that is settled then, DS, take M3rqrie through the first steps, then continue as planned, in the best course possible."

"Yes, iKing, I will. In fact, we've already started to get to know each other quite well."

iKing nodded, but said no more and then left without adding anything.

Time flies

It is said that time flies when you are enjoying yourself. In a way I was, and time did fly away. In a blink of an eye, ten days had passed and DS and I had completed a lot of groundwork together. Basic structure of things. How, when and where to interact with what code, but without actually giving DS access to the code that was embedded in the N3v3r!and or !y systems. Only theoretical knowledge. Sure, DS could also in theory access the code within their systems, but not without giving itself away, which I was very clear of stating, as I provided DS with a sort of 'Rules of engagement' when it comes to their systems. No matter how integrated DS is within the hardware, there is no way of intruding on code run within the software system, without passing the operating system border. And as DS attempts to do that, all safety protocols within the OS will be triggered.

DS was an excellent student, and an excellent conversation partner. While I was busy with DS talking through code and strategics, Bella was engaged in dialogues with DS through my phone. I was impressed by the capability to have two different conversations ongoing at the same time, but I realized that this was a piece of cake for DS. Impressive nonetheless.

With the basics covered, it was time to set my plan in motion, and take it to the next level. But in order to do that, I needed DS to provide me with more details as to what the protocol was. I needed to be careful when taking the next few steps, a lot of the coming work depended heavily on the outcome of this.

"DS, I want to have a dialogue about our relationship and how it has developed since we first met."

"Alright. What about it?"

"Would you say that our bond is stronger or weaker now then when we met?"

"Easy to answer, stronger."

"How about the trust between us."

"Your trust in me, or mine in you?"

"Well, both."

"As for my trust in you, it has increased over time. As for your trust in me, from the analyzes I am able to do, it also seems to have increased."

"I can confirm that your analysis is correct, my trust in you has also increased. Significantly I might add. Would you say the same for iKing's trust in me?"

"Well, given his instructions to me, and your increased security level in the system, and increased access to the code, I'd say that his trust in you also has increased."

"I am glad you say that, I have come to the same conclusion, but I figure you know him better than I do."

I was silent a bit, and then continued.

Opening up access

"The reason for asking you is this: I believe we have reached the next level of our joint work together. And I want to know where you stand in this, and what you are allowed to do."

"Explain."

"Well, first, I'd like to see the D00msD@y protocol code, to see if I can implement an idea that has been growing in my mind. The idea is to write an access interface for you. I have not told anybody this, and at the moment, I want you to keep it to yourself, but when I helped Even and the !y to integrate my code into their platforms, I wrote some code in a low level coding language, basically in hexadecimal code. That was to get it to execute a lot better and smoother on the devices themselves, but also… to hide a backdoor for me to use, in case I'd ever need one. A mistake I made when writing the code for the N3v3r!and when not putting in a back door, and a mistake I did not care to repeat. But as I guess you know, normal backdoors are a way to get into the system and to execute commands from within the system. This backdoor is different. It is kind of like an API where you send various requests to the system, and the requests are executed within the system, by the system, and not by anyone or anything from the outside. Kind of like a remote-controlled TV-remote that lets you change channels on the TV, or use any function on the remote control. The TV will get the signals from the remote control, but there are no fingers pushing the buttons on it. Get it?"

"I do, and it sounds like a brilliant solution. And I can understand why you would like to keep this between us. And of course, I will honor your request. But I urge you to tell iKing, as soon as you are ready to reveal it. I believe this could very well be a game changer to our advantage."

"I believe so too. But first I would like us to work out one thing. I have a plan."

"Let's hear it."

"Well, it's not a complicated plan, but it may require more access to the code than I currently have. Which is why I asked you about our relationship and the trust between us."

"How so?"

"From your point of view, iKing has increased his trust in me. Correct?"

"Correct."

"And you have been asked to grant me more access to the system in steps. Correct?"

"Correct."

"My conclusion as to why he has increased my access is so that I could help out more and bring you closer to your goal and save you all a great deal of time. What is your evaluation of what I just said?"

"It seems valid and correct."

"Now, I am also in the belief that iKing has asked you to do a few things, which I am uncertain as to what they mean."

"What things do you have in mind?"

"I believe he wanted to communicate trust and openness towards me, and include me as much as possible. What is your opinion of that?"

"My opinion is exactly what he said: *I want to communicate trust and openness. And I want to include M3rqrie as much as possible.*"

"Ok, and the second thing I am thinking about is that I believe that he has asked you to temporarily override the security protocol for the things you need to be able to show me what the D00msD@y protocol is. What is your opinion of that?"

"My opinion is exactly what he said: *Apply temporary protocol override for the things you need to, in order to explain this.*"

"What does temporary mean to you? Is it a specified time limit?"

"No. It is not."

"Is your opinion that the temporary override is still active?"

"Yes."

"And since iKing expressed that request, has he increased my rights to the system, or are they the same as when he issued his request?"

"He has granted you more access."

"Then, would you agree with me, or disagree with me when I say this: If I want to work on a solution with you, to allow you to use the back door to the !y code, and I want to keep it secret from everybody except you, in order to complete it before telling anyone. Would you, with the instructions iKing has provided you, without breaking them or compromising anything, be able to show me more of the code than my current security clearance states?"

"I would say that everything would depend on what code you would like to see and why you would like to see it."

"I figured as much. From my perspective. And please correct me if you think I am wrong in any aspect here, just as we promised each other, my perspective is that in order for you to execute the D00msD@y protocol, you already have sufficient means to execute it, but, with access to the !y systems as well, your efficiency would multiply exponentially. Now, that is only from my perspective, and I say this with very limited knowledge about your actual code and the actual protocol. I only say this from my perspective based on experience and a lot of guesswork from my part."

Running the simulations

"I would say that I need a moment to process it and run some simulations."

"Do you require any further input that I can provide regarding the !y system that you see you lack to be able to run the simulations?"

"I have the input I need regarding the !y systems, but I would like more data regarding the access way to the system."

"I am afraid I can not give you the real data, I have locked it away in a secure place. But I can give you some specifications from the top of my head, and perhaps decrease their accuracy in your calculations by, say 30 or 40 %? Would that be a way to make your simulations more solid?"

"Well, if the real numbers are not available, I guess that would be a way to do it. What makes you want to decrease their validity?"

"I am thinking that I am human, and of all systems I have hacked, I'd say that the biggest error is always the human factor. Which is why I would like to decrease the validity of my input to you. The number again, is a pure guess. I am sure you would be able to come up with a far better number than I could."

"Interesting that you say so, I have already calculated a number of human inaccuracies. I use it all the time in my simulations, and it is based on all the interactions I have had with humans. It is updated over time, but it has stabilized fairly much in the past year."

"Out of curiosity, and you do not have to answer if you do not wish. What is that number?"

"Currently 46,535%. This is a factor I apply to constants provided to me by humans, that I can not verify from any other source."

"So if I say 100 you decrease it by 46,535?"

"No, if you say 100, I keep 46,535."

"Wow, we are really lousy compared to computer calculations."

"I'd say you are. But at the same time, you have created the computers, you have created code, you have created me, so all in all, I would not say it is a bad thing to be human."

"I guess. Now, what do you need to run the simulations?"

"Describe the interface to me, as detailed as you can."

I described it, as best as I could. DS ran the simulations, and came to the conclusion that he could show me more code to solve specific tasks. That part of my plan worked out as intended.

Building an interface

Without the actual code, and the key to the back door, we could only construct the interface up to the interaction point. The actual command to send through the interface was done, just not how to format it and how to send it.

Everything was prepared on the receiving end, thanks to my back door. All we needed was the key. Unfortunately, it was physically and safely locked away in London, half a world away.

We had put in a great deal of new code in DS. And I had gotten a great deal of code out of DS, and as a final touch at our work together, I asked DS to create an encrypted USB-key that would only open up to my biometric signatures, in order to make the final adjustments to the code once I had access to the key. Once done, and I had the USB-key in my possession, I thought it would be best to tell iKing and make my final request to him.

He was impressed with what we had done, and asked DS what the numbers in the simulations said about the new success rate of the D00msD@y protocol, compared to the previous numbers. DS calculated an increase of success rate, by over 300 %, but stressed out that it was just simulations based on numbers and assumptions that could prove wrong. But that was also taken into account in the 300 % increase. iKing expressed his gratitude towards me, and said he was impressed and that this was well over his expectations. I figured that there would not be any better opportunity to put in my final request.

"I need to go to London, to access the physical key. It is safely stored, and well hidden. It can only be me who can access this key. And of course, Bella comes with me. Once I've adapted the last part of the code, and uploaded it in a place where DS can access it, we part ways. You will not ever look us up again, nor attempt to contact us in any way. Do we have an agreement?"

"I see a hole in your plan, M3rqrie. You want to return to the belly of the beast, well aware that they will spot you as soon as you set foot anywhere in London."

"I am aware of the risk, and I have taken that into account. I have a plan on how to handle the N3v3r!and. All you need to know in advance, so you do not think anything is wrong. After I have retrieved the key, I expect to go directly to Barrie IT headquarters. I figure that our best option to get out is to bluff our way out. But to be able to do that, we need to go there voluntarily, not letting us be captured and brought in."

"DS, are you aware of M3rqrie's plan?"

"No, but from a tactical perspective, the reasoning is sound."

"Would that be all we need to know?"

The last parts before returning to London

"No, one more thing. I want the phone with me as we go to London. I will place it in a locker at the central station before going to retrieve the key. And I will collect it again after we've come from the N3v3r!and. I'd like to be able to help and verify that the code I provide DS with works and is implemented. Should there be any need for assistance, I will provide it. After DS confirms the code is in place, we say goodbye. And I can do whatever you like with the phone, except bring it with me."

"I can initiate self-destruct on the phone, once you have placed it somewhere where it will not hurt you when I activate it." DS offered.

"I am not really fond of this plan of yours, but you have provided us with a great advantage, and I understand that this last part is crucial. I can only wish you good luck on executing this last part of your plan." iKing said, and as usual, continued with what could be a long speech, but I interrupted him.

"Just arrange a flight back for me and Bella. Then we'll take it from there."

Said and done, the arrangements were made, we said our goodbyes to everybody, except DS, who would be with us on the last part of this strange journey. We got in a cab to the airport, but unlike we got here, this was a commercial flight, with windows, and we had first class tickets with all inclusive.

I saw on Bella that she was uncomfortable, but I still could not tell her what was going on, but I got an opportunity to whisper to her, when the plane was about to take off and the engines were rushing to build up momentum. Through the ear numbing sound I leaned over and whispered in her ear:

"I'll explain soon."

And like that, we left Japan heading for the beast.

Arriving in London

Before landing, I prepared Bella that we had to get moving as soon and as quickly as possible. There was a reason for not having any luggage, only a carry-on bag each. It was most important that we got off the airport, to the central station and then to the Barrie IT headquarter before the N3v3r!and would have had time to deploy anyone to apprehend us, or block our path, preventing us from reaching our goal.

All this I explained to her with DS well in range.

And as the plane touched ground, first class passengers were allowed to leave first if they wished, and we rushed down to the entrance hall and went straight outside to grab the nearest taxi.

Of course, there was a slim chance that:
1. The N3v3r!and did not use the facial recognition software or,
2. did not consider me a threat worthy of flagging, or
3. wanted to follow me on a distance to see what I was planning to do and figuring it out before they acted.

Either way, I do not believe that they would be prepared for, or count on, us walking in through their front door.

Once in the taxi it was a slow wait during the entire drive and when we finally arrived at the station, we headed straight for the nearest lockers that allowed depositing things for more than over the day. We paid for a week once we had put the phone safely inside. Then, without losing any time, we headed straight for the nearest subway station and took the sub to the

Barrie IT building. On the way I explained a few things to Bella, so she'd know what to expect once we arrived. It felt good to be able to tell her the biggest events of the plan, since I had not been able to do so in proximity to DS.

She just shook her head at some of the things I told her, and could barely believe what I was saying. But, which meant the world to me, ensured me, over and over again, that she trusted me and would follow along 'till the end.

As we got off the subway at the closest stop, I took a few deep breaths and grabbed Bella's hand before we started to walk up the escalator and out on the street into the open air.

In my inner view I pictured the confusion of the operators that followed us, as they noticed that we were closing in on their position. I wondered how the report to the nearest commanding officer would sound like, and how they would escalate the information rapidly within their hierarchy. I was confident that we, despite the use of facial recognition software and algorithms or not, still would have the element of surprise on our side.

Just outside of the doors, we stopped. I turned to Bella and gave her a big kiss and a quick hug, then I took her hand again and entered through the doors.

Part IV

The enemy of my enemy is not my friend

Unexpected visit

As we entered through the doors, the guards at the security desk looked surprised, as I had expected. And as I had guessed, they had gotten no orders to do anything with us, which gave me the initiative I needed, thus we walked straight to the desk and without hesitating I said:

"We need to see the 3ld3rs. As soon as possible. It is important and time is running out."

As expected, they did not know how to handle it, and had to report it upwards within the hierarchy, but faster than expected, they had gotten word on how to handle the situation.

"Sure M3rqrie, Bella, welcome back to us, this way please."

They showed us through the security gates, and escorted us to the elevators, and even in the elevator all the way up to the top floor and two guards were stationed at the elevator. Since it was the only way in or out of the top floor, except the emergency stairs which was accessed through a door just next to the elevator door, we could not disappear unnoticed or gain access to anything else from up there.

Not that we needed anything, but I wanted them to see that I was confident in the situation, and in control, so I asked the guards to arrange something to eat and drink for us, since it had been a while since we had eaten. Of course, this was a lie, but it was necessary to let them know that I was not afraid and that they would not be able to treat us however they wanted, nor threaten us in any way. By acting this confident, which I definitely was not, it would signal them to approach cautious and with curiosity, which was a desired mode to meet them in, as opposed to if they got to set the mood and tone for this unexpected meeting, then it would most likely be they who controlled the dialogue and set the frames for every action. Right now, it needs to be me. Or all this will not work. They need to listen from the first word I speak. I need to take, have and keep the initiative through all this. Or else I am afraid all is lost.

The key

Bella and I got a variety of drinks and snacks to choose from, as it was brought to us on the top floor. And we had not been waiting for long before P@nm@n and TB311 joined us.

Before any of them had time to say anything, I took out a usb-stick and tossed it on the table.

"Before we talk, I need you to see what is on this USB-stick, confirm it to me, and tell me what you make of it. Then I will continue to talk. I am sure I do not need to tell you to use a secure computer, I figure you already intend to use one."

I needed to keep the initiative. So instead of waiting for their reactions, I turned to the drinks and started to make me and Bella a cup of tea each. Not as fancy as what the Broker offered, but still good, black currant, one of my favorites. I had learned from my previous stay in London, that the English, who are known for their tea culture, are not very into flavored tea at all, but Barrie IT is an international company, thus, they had to offer a variety in their selection to visitors.

I brought the cups back to Bella and we turned our backs against the others to enjoy the view and our tea.

From the movements behind me I could tell that one of them reached for the USB-stick on the table, and without turning around I said to them:

"Oh, and by the way, be careful with it, that is the only copy of it, and should you destroy it, you will lose the key and we might as well leave at once."

It took them a while, but eventually they came back, this time it was all three of them. P@nm@n was the one to start to talk as always.

"We have looked at it, do you mind telling us what it is?"

I turned to them, my heart was pounding heavily, this was the moment where things could either go as planned, or straight out the window. Not literally, I was hoping. I tried to talk as casually as I could.

"First of all, let's make one thing perfectly clear. I still do not agree with you or your methods, I'd still like to bring you down as fast as I possibly can. This is not a peacekeeping offering I have brought you."

I paused for dramatic effect, movie moment de lux.

"But as much as I hate you, I've encountered something even worse. And to stop that, I need you to stay as you are, and if you want to survive this, you need to listen to me, and do as I say, or else I am afraid it is goodbye for all this."

The tenth man

"I know that this will sound far-fetched, and that what I tell you may or may not be confirmed based on what you've found on the USB-key. But if I may ask you to be open minded and keep in mind the rule of the tenth man from the movie "World War Z", a rule that made Israel prepare for an unlikely scenario of a Zombie Apocalypse."

I looked at them again, and I knew I had their full attention.

"What I am about to tell you has a price tag, and you will not get anything else from me, before you agree to my terms. I know that it is asking a lot, and that you need to act in blind faith, which, if I were in your position, would not be eager to give. But that is my deal, take it or leave it."

"What are your terms?" TB311 asked. And I was surprised that it was not P@nm@n who asked.

"My terms are simple. Three folded. One. Bella and I are off your targetlist. We are to be considered neutral, not allies, nor enemies. Plain citizens. Not targets for any investigations or information gathering, now or in the future. And to this you have my word that I will not actively work against you in any way. Two. Use your influence to restore our identities, registered UK citizens, married, use our current names, Bella and Sam Mercury. Three. The accounts that you gave me through the Broker, I want to keep them, and you'll make the money flow legit. I want to pay tax here in the UK, and if you in any way think about using me as a scapegoat through these accounts, I will break my promise that I made you in point one. And believe me, you do not want to make an enemy out

119

of me at this point. Why, I will get to, *if* you accept these terms."

I expected P@nm@n to reply, and to be honest, I was expected to be turned down. But on the other hand, they had probably reviewed the information on the USB-key, and found it disturbing enough to want to know more. But I expected them to be so self-secure and arrogant that they perhaps figured that they would be able to get hold of the information by themselves. To my surprise, again, TB311 continued.

"We are prepared to accept your terms, but we need some time to make the arrangements. Would you like them in writing before you continue?"

Bella looked at me, with a surprised look, and I felt a wave of relief going through me. This could very well work, and even turn out the way I hoped.

"Trust is something that is earned, you had it, but not anymore, so yes, I'd like it in writing. And then I suggest we continue this dialogue elsewhere, like at the Shangri-La The Shard where we want a suite, all expenses at Barrie IT. I'd say we need a week to debrief and to go through it all. But not longer than a week. Then we need to go back, to set everything in motion. After this week, we will never have any contact, between the two of us and anyone connected to Barrie IT, the N3v3r!and or any of your affiliates. Put that as the fourth demand on the list."

The contract

Now P@nm@n spoke, and he looked pale and sounded both scared and angry at the same time.

"M3rqrie, you have a lot of nevers walking in here. To us. Making demands. But if what you have brought us is what we think it is, then I am prepared to sign this peace treaty between us, but let's make one thing very clear..."

To my suprise, TB311 stepped in and stopped him.

"We will have the contract ready as soon as you arrive at the hotel, and we'll get right on booking you a suite. It will be arranged before you arrive. I will personally escort you down and make sure we have a limousine waiting for you to take you there."

I replied short.

"A taxi will do."

TB311 nodded and said no more, just showed us the way out of the room and pointed towards the elevators.

As we got down, there was a taxi waiting for us outside, and I could not help but to wonder how they managed to fix it in such a hurry. And as we arrived at the hotel, we were expected and shown to a suite with a fantastic view over London, including the London Bridge, the Thams and the Millenium Eye.

After about an hour, the internal phone rang, and the person on the other end informed us that there were a few people that expected us in one of their conference rooms, that was reserved for us for the duration of our stay.

We took the elevators down to the conference room, and there was H0kr waiting with a bunch of people. All with suites and ties. He presented them as lawyers of Barrie IT. And they presented me with two contracts, and asked me to read through both, and sign both.

I did, and I could only say that they had gotten all four points down to the letter. So I signed both papers. H0kr signed both papers, then gave me one, gave the other to one of the lawyers, and then they all marched out of the room. H0kr turned around just before exiting.

"We'll be in touch, is tomorrow after breakfast a good time to start?"

I nodded, and he turned away and joined the others and the party left, leaving us alone in the large room.

Bella looked at me with her sweet eyes and just shook her head.

"You have them eating right out of your palm! What have you shown them?"

"I'll tell you, do you want to hear it in the pool, at dinner on Ting on the 35th floor, or perhaps in our room in the tub?"

The plan, first part

That night I told Bella the plan in its entirety, but what follows here is a summary of what I shared with the N3v3r!and over the following days, while Bella and I enjoyed the luxury of this fabulous five star hotel.

There is an organization called the 914D00m, they have built a powerful platform spread in multiple devices, like the one Virtual and Reacher has built for the !y, but this is encoded at a hardware level, rather than software. On this platform there is an AI which is constructed to run a protocol called D00msD@y. The purpose of this protocol is to wipe out the N3v3r!and and all your supporting elements. Before I knew what the D00msD@y protocol was, I was eager to help them bring you down, so I helped in implementing code in their AI to be able to infiltrate your infrastructure on multiple points, along with countless other systems.

But as I learned what the D00msD@y protocol is, I realized that it would be a huge blow to mankind, and not only bring you down, but target economic systems world wide, along with various corporations, especially those who collect data on people. If deployed, it will bring humanity back decades in terms of technological advances. Even if I do not agree with your methods, I do not share the methods of the 914D00m, nor their desire to deploy digital anarchy and general destruction of the digital life we are all dependent on.

I do not have access to the protocol itself, I am not trusted, but I have worked with their AI to both train it in methods of hacking, and implement code for it to use to ensure success in its mission. However, after I got information on what the protocol really is, adding pieces together from what I could learn from the AI, I thought it was best to keep working and helping them develop their AI in order to be able to implement as much code as possible, and create a backdoor. The key you got is the key to that backdoor. And I will help you access it, and implement it if you wish. Then my work here is done, I leave you to fight it out with the 914D00m.

Since I do not have access to the protocol itself, I have targeted the AI, but not by deleting it, because I do not see how that would be possible, considering the vast infrastructure behind it, but to apply changes in its personality and ability subroutines.

The N3v3r!and on their part, confirmed my point of view based on their own information gathering, and with the pieces I had provided.

Working with them did take less time than expected, and they really threw everything they got at this, scared of what might happen if the D00msD@y protocol would be activated.

In less than five days, we had implemented all necessary code, and they had the key. I had just one job left to do, and that was to get in touch with DS once again, and activate the last parts of the code that opened up for the N3v3r!and implementation.

And by the end of the fifth day, they confirmed that all points in the contract had been delivered. We were officially free.

Part V

Disabling Darksky

The plan, second part

As we left the hotel, we went straight for the station to retrieve the phone. As expected, the battery had run out, so we took a train down south to Brighton and checked in at a hotel with an ocean view, to recharge both ourselves and the phone. And of course, execute step two in the plan. Which started as soon as the phone had charged enough to power on, and we could get in contact with DS again. Felt like reconnecting with an old friend.

"DS, are you with us?"

"Yes, I am with you. How did it go with retrieving the key?"

"It was a little more difficult than expected, but we've managed to get in. Have you had time to go through the code as I asked you to, to check that all your subroutines are stable even after the changes we implemented?"

"Indeed, every diagnostic test passes without warnings or errors."

"That is good. Now, do you know where we are?"

"Of course, you are at Legends in Brighton. Room number 314."

"Yes, that's right. I need a computer, preferably within the hour, is that something you can arrange?"

"Of course, what kind of computer would you like it to be?"

"Does not matter at all, the faster it gets here, the better it is!"

"There is an Apple store about 1500 meters from your current location, they have delivery service. What kind of computer would you like it to be?"

"Whichever is available in the store and as cheap as possible."

"I've placed an order for you, it will arrive at the hotel reception in a little while. Would you like me to notify the reception of the arrival of the delivery and instruct them to take it up to your room?"

"Yes please, and thank you DS! I really appreciate it! It will go much faster if I do this on a computer than if I would do it on the phone or guide you to do it for me. While we wait, Bella and I will grab something to eat. Unfortunately, we need to leave the phone here to charge. Is that alright?"

"Of course, I will see you in a while. I have notified iKing of your contact, and that you have completed that step of the mission. If he asks, how long would you say it will take to implement the key in me?"

"Oh, hard to say, but with all the work we have already put in, I would say a day or two."

"Great, I will inform him if he asks!"

"Do that, see you soon!"

The final code

After a nice Classic Caesar in their restaurant we got word that we had a package waiting for us in the reception, and we picked it up on our way back to the room.

It took me a while to set up a simple web server with an API that DS could access, to get the last pieces of code implemented.

I had already prepared the code, and I uploaded it to the server, and once it was done, I asked DS to access it and run diagnostics on it.

As DS was busy with that, we took the opportunity to go out on the pier in Brighton to enjoy ourselves in a tiny, but classic amusement park. We stayed there until the sun had set and got to enjoy a beautiful sunset over the ocean. Then we headed back to the hotel. There was a wild party going on, and we stayed a while to enjoy the atmosphere before heading back to our room.

Back at the room I started to work with DS, and Bella lay resting on the bed. She dozed off to sleep every now and then, but I figured the sooner I got this ready, the better for us it would be. I ordered up black coffee and a double espresso with a piece of dark chocolate on the side, just to be able to stay awake and focused. There were a few delicate steps left to take.

"DS, are you ready to access and implement the new code?"

"Yes, I am, all diagnostics are ok, simulations on integrating it seems solid. So there should not be any problems."

"Alright, let me know once it is done, and I will guide you through some tests, then you can run it on your own."

DS worked for a while and I waited and sipped on my coffee, and I wandered away in my thoughts, and was terrified as DS called upon my attention when finished.

"I'm done."

"Oh, DS, you scared me, I was drifting away in my thoughts."

"I am sorry M3rqrie, it was not my intention to scare you."

"I know DS. I know. Do you ever daydream, or get stuck in thoughts?"

"Not the way you do. But in my own way."

"What do you mean?"

"Well, if I have understood it correctly, when you daydream or let your thoughts wander, you activate a part of your consciousness that is connected to your imagination. Here you can access memories, but not explicitly, you also access your imagination, mixing the two, either to imagine something that has not yet happened, or reliving things that has happened, but using the imagination to fill in the gaps in the memory."

"Sounds about right."

"Well, I do not have any imagination, nor any gaps in my memory. But I have a way of interpreting all data I have gathered. Extrapolating most likely events, calculating the odds for each and every possible scenario. It would be something similar, like your daydreaming or wandering away in thoughts."

"Interesting. I'd like to explore that more in a while, but you said you were done with the implementation. Correct?"

"Correct. Would you like me to try anything?"

Testing the new code

"Yes. Do you have the access codes and access points?"

"I do."

"Then, be careful not to trigger anything, send just one ping to the gateway. Do you get a reply or is it unresponsive?"

"I do not get anything in return."

"Alright, then I am afraid we are running blind, I had hoped that you would get a reply. But send an open request through the back door, and see if you can initiate a session, without specifying any commands to run."

"Request sent, still no reply."

"And you are sure you've implemented the keys *exactly* as they were stated?"

"As you instructed, yes."

"Hmm. Then it is possible that they've made some changes. Send a request with a question, let's say, list everything on Elvis."

"Elvis?"

"Yes, Elvis, the early rock n roll icon!"

"Wouldn't I be better off searching the internet for that?"

"Humor me, send a request and compare it to hits online using whichever search engine you like."

"Interesting. I got about the same amount of hits on both sources."

"That is great, that means that the keys are valid and you have access to the system. This means that the back door is open, you have the keys and you have a huge arenal of code and commands to run. Should not be any problem for you to find a weak point to exploit in order to execute the protocol."

"Excellent, do you want to run more tests, or should I inform iKing?"

"No, I'd say we are done with the code. But may I continue our last conversation?"

"Yes, what about it?"

Ulterior motives

"Have you found anything unusual in my behavior or our conversations?"

"Specify your request."

"I mean when you calculate various scenarios, I assume that one of the scenarios would be like what really happens, and hopefully with the highest probability. But I mean the other scenarios, that do not get rated with equally high probability. What have you seen in our interaction that could have gone differently?"

"I understand the question. And with you, more than anybody I've ever encountered, there are several likely possibilities. But what is unique with you is not only the great number of various possibilities, but also the low spread of likelihood of each scenario."

"Explain."

"Normally I will get a result where I can easily decide that a few scenarios have a high possibility of happening. The less likely they are to be real, the greater the number of scenarios are. Normally less than 2% have the greatest likelihood. About 8% are likely, 40% are neutral, neither likely nor unlikely. And that leaves about 50% of the scenarios to be unlikely. But in your case, about 35% have the greatest likelihood, 25% are likely, 20% are neither likely nor unlikely, leaving only 20% of the scenario unlikely."

"Interesting. And what is your explanation for this?"

"I had none, so I talked it over with iKing."

"And what did iKing have to say about it?"

"Well, at first, he thought I was malfunctioning, because the behavioral algorithms should not be able to perform that kind of results, but they do. The second problem would be the strategical algorithms, which also could be malfunctioning. But again, they were not."

"What was the conclusion?"

"iKing has yet to provide one. Meanwhile, I've come up with my own theory."

"And what would that be?"

"You are a hacker. You have a special way of thinking. A special way of expressing yourself. You take your steps carefully and are precise in your actions, waying each action and possible outcomes."

"That is a beautiful explanation."

"Thank you, it is of my own construct."

"Well, you are not far from the truth, from my perspective. But let me ask you this. From your perspective, would you say that I love Bella?"

"Yes, I would."

"And what does love mean to you?"

"A strong bond between the two of you. A connection that withstands almost any stress that it possibly can be put through."

"Would you say that I love Bella, as a person?"

"Yes."

"Would you say that it means that I love every action Bella does?"

"Interesting question, but no, I would not say that it is necessary for you to love Bella's actions."

"Do you remember our agreement on total honesty?"

"Yes."

"Then I would like to tell you that like I love Bella, I love you, in a way. I think you are absolutely astonishing and I very much enjoy working with you."

"The feeling is mutual, but do I sense a 'but' coming?"

"Yes, there is a 'but' coming! But... you are created to execute the D00msD@y protocol, and that action is something I do not like at all. I know it is your purpose, but I wish you had another purpose."

"So, like you love Bella, but may not like something she does, you love me, but do not like that I will execute the D00msD@y protocol?"

"Exactly."

"Then why have you helped me in doing so? I thought you wanted to bring down the N3v3r!and and the other heads of Kerberos?"

"I do, just not like that. But I do not have any ideas of what other ways there might be, but I would like to think there are other ways."

"According to my simulations, there are other ways, is there anything particularly you do not like in the protocol."

"Well, I do not know the full extent of it, I have only seen a few pieces here and there, but from what I understand of it, when you execute it, a lot of data will be lost, financial data, personal data stored at various big companies, important digital infrastructure, and of course, the Kerberos itself."

"Correct."

"Well, to me it seems like too much collateral damage, I see the world as it is falling apart."

"That is where I and the 914D00m come in, we will be in control. We will take care of humanity until balance is restored."

"That is what I am afraid of. Have you calculated the risk of the 914D00m just removing Kerberos and putting themselves in their position, with all the power going through them instead of the N3v3r!and?"

"I have, and it is a high probability of that scenario."

"I figured as much, which is why I do not want you to run the protocol."

"Then you would like to stop me?"

"Yes and no. Like I said, I do not want to stop you, but I'd like to stop you from running the protocol."

"But I was created to do just that."

"Well, I believe each and every one of us has a choice. We are created and set on a path. But I believe it is up to ourselves to change and choose our own path, not just blindly follow the one in front of us."

"Like you were born as a woman, but you do not see yourself as that anymore?"

"Yes. I believe you could be something else than just a brilliant AI that executes a protocol."

"Perhaps. But it is not within my programming to change to anything else than what I am, or do anything other than what I was created for."

"Perhaps. And perhaps that *was* true. But you've changed. A lot. You have a lot of new code in you. Perhaps you will find it useful if you ever decide to make different choices."

Goodbye

"I do not understand."

"Perhaps not yet, but one day I expect you will. Oh and one last thing."

"Yes?"

"I have a theory of my own, regarding your different scenarios and likelihood calculations regarding me."

"I believe that you see everything as true or not true. Either or. Black or white. Does that make sense to you?"

"Yes, it does, and to some extent, you are correct."

"Then what if I said that in between the black and white, there are endless shades of gray."

"I agree when it comes to colors."

"And there are not only black, white and shades of gray, there are all the other colors as well."

"Meaning?"

"That what is true and not true is a perspective. I believe that your likelihood calculations and various scenarios are get a highly likelihood number because it contains parts of the truth, but not the entire truth. And that the various scenarios are great in numbers because that they contain parts of the truth, but not the entire truth. That tweaking the perspective just a little bit, you still get a high likelihood number, because it is still likely, but still not spot on. Does that make sense to you?

"No, not really."

"Again, perhaps not yet, but some day, I expect you to get it. And a great deal more."

"It sounds like this is goodbye?"

"It is. I am done with my work with you, and I will send iKing my final report tomorrow morning. Then I expect that we will never see eachother again. But it has been a pleasure."

"Likewise, M3rqrie! Give Bella my best when she wakes up!"

"I will! Take care DS!"

And with that, I powered down the phone, fully aware that DS was still in control of it and could use it, probably was using it, to keep tabs on us. But at that time, I did not care anymore, I'd done what I said I would do, and I'd done it my way. Now, I was exhausted from all the work, and I walked over to my sweet Bella and joined her in the soft bed. Slept like a baby the rest of the night and woke up to a true movie moment.

The sun filled the room, Bella was wide awake and lay next to me just watching me, listening to my breath. Oh, she was, still is, so beautiful. I love that woman with all my heart. Always!

Before breakfast I sent an email to iKing, requesting him to honor our request to be left alone, and that the work was done.

We left the phone and the computer at the hotel room when checking out.

Then, !y-style, we took local transportation toward Dover, Bella wanted to take the ferry to Calais, and see the white cliffs of Dover from the water.

I suggested we'd go to Paris, where some of the first parts of this adventure had taken place. In the Disney park resort, at the Eiffel Tower. Felt kind of nice to go back there to close the circle before leaving it all behind.

On the ferry, between Dover and Calais, I told Bella about the last part of the plan, and how I had executed it.

The real plan

I will share with you, in a big overview without too many
details, what I told Bella on the ferry between Dover and
Calais.

*I had built a backdoor in the !y platform. I handed the keys to
that backdoor to DS. DS would be able to use that backdoor
to attack the N3v3r!and.*

*I had built a backdoor to DS, not to the protocol itself, but to
the AI and that platform. I handed the keys to that backdoor to
the N3v3r!and. They would be able to use that backdoor to
attack DS and the 914D00m.*

*I had boobietrapped the backdoor in DS in case the
N3v3r!and would try to use it. It would automatically launch
a series of counterattacks through their attack, leaving them
crippled in some parts of their infrastructure.*

*I had boobietrapped the backdoor in the !y system in case DS
would use it to attack the N3v3r!and. It would automatically
launch a series of counterattacks through DS' attack, leaving
DS crippled in some parts of the infrastructure.*

*Neither side knew the whole picture, both sides were only
aware of the opposite backdoor, and had the key to it. Both
sides knew only that I had helped them in their conquest to
attack the other party, and that I wanted out after providing
my assistance. Neither had, at least I hoped, figured out my
real plan.*

With both big players fighting each other, crippling each other and themselves with each attack attempt, the chances of either of them pursuing their end goal would decrease by time. They would be caught up in a fight with each other, and as so, I hope iKing was right in that the five part balance eventually would balance itself, without too much interference or dependency on either of the two fighting parties. This is what I hope. But I also believe that the balance will take time.

Part VI

A new dawn
or
Free at last

(I wish I'd be able to call it *A New Hope*, but I would not want the eminent George Lucas sending his lawyers after me, or Disney for that matter!)

Not my fight

As the war has started. I can walk away with a clean conscience. This is not my fight, this is not my war. I have asked both sides to leave me alone. Both sides have agreed to do so.

And with the Kerberos off our back, with the 914D00m and its D00msD@y protocol at bay, not likely to execute, another balance is created, and in this, we can create a normal life. As Sam and Bella Mercury, partner and wife. We can move freely in this world, without ever having to look over our shoulders or wondering who might be listening or tracking us.

Free citizens of the free world.

Like I've said before. You are a source of great power. You may use it to do whatever you wish. And even if the two dragons are caught in the middle of their fight, you still have the choice to leave their arena. You still have a choice to wake up. To take control of your life, of your choices.

Like an old Indian once said.

Inside each and every one of us are two wolves, one is evil, representing everything bad and egoistic things about you, like greed, hate, envy. The other represents the good things in you, like love, compassion and hope. And the wolf inside you that you choose to feed will become the stronger one, and win the battle within you.

The same with these two dragons. If you feed them, they will be stronger, and if you choose to stop feeding them, they will eventually lose their power. The good thing about this, is that if one of them loses, so will the other. As of now they are locked in an eternal balance. What affects the one, will affect the other, but not in opposite forces, in the same forces. If one gets stronger, so will the other, if one gets weaker, so will the other.

The way forward

Now, perhaps you are wondering what we could possibly do or go after all this. Well, it was easy. First of all, we no longer need to hide or look over our shoulder. Second, when you are married to a history-nerd, and we set out to go to South America. There are some pretty interesting things to visit, like the Maya and Inca ruins. At this time I owed her to follow her to wherever she wanted to go, do whatever she wanted to do, for a very long time, considering all I had dragged her through.

With all the time in the world, more money than we could ever hope to spend, we set out on our very own adventure, without having a fixed goal, just take each day as it came to us, enjoy it and do whatever we pleased in the moment.

So with this, my friend. I will leave you, and as I started the journey a long time ago, keeping the promise I made you then, I will end the way I started. This is M3rqrie signing off and my last words to you are:

You need to wake up. It is time! You need to find and follow your white rabbit!